Andie

"Step by step. One foot in front of the other. The sun will rise, and the tides will change."

Sending love + hugs

Rachel
De Lune

x

New Tides

RACHEL DE LUNE

Ellie Carter is hiding, living a half-life and nursing scars that never healed. Abandoning her job and her family, she fled to the coast and hoped to escape her memories and pain. But she's haunted by both.

Owen Riggs is the eternal optimist, so when he breaks what little trust Ellie had in him, he knows he can earn it back.

Step by step, touch by touch, he works to repair the damage he's caused. But no matter how deeply in love Owen falls, he learns that the scars you can't see are the hardest to heal.

©All rights reserved. No part of this book may be reproduced without written consent from the author, except that of small quotations used in critical reviews and promotions via blogs.

New Tides is a work of fiction. Names, characters, businesses, places, events and incidents are either the products of the author's imagination or used in a fictitious manner. Any resemblance to actual persons, living or dead, or actual events is purely coincidental.

New Tides ©2018 Rachel De Lune
Cover design by LJDesigns
Book design by LJDesigns
Editing by Claire Allmendinger and Rox Leblanc
Rachel De Lune on Social Media:
Facebook: www.facebook.com/racheldeluneauthor/
Instagram: www.instagram.com/racheldeluneauthor
Website: www.racheldelune.com

ACKNOWLEDGEMENTS

Cornwall is one of my favourite places in the world. I've been visiting it all of my life and have so many special memories there. And as I thought about writing this story, there was no question where it would be set. New Tides, became as much about Cornwall as it did about the characters. It's my firm opinion that everyone should visit Cornwall at least once.

I am unbelievably fortunate to have some wonderful and amazing people in my life that support me every step of the way. Thanking each of you from the bottom of my heart. Elizabeth Safleur, Kris Micheals, Marilyn Lakewood, Madeline Iva, Charlotte Hart, Grace Harper and Becky Prescott.

My list continues with some talented people that I'm also lucky enough to call friends. Lou, for such a stunning cover. You blow me away each and every time. Claire, for ensuring my words are fit for consumption, and for everything you do with Wendy at BNW. And Rox for your keen eye.

My last word of thanks goes to three readers who received ARCs of New Tides. This was a very different story to what I've released before, and so I was riddled with nerves as to how people were going to feel about this story. I always my version of the story in my head, but that's not necessarily the correct or popular decision. Thank you to Lori, Julie and Lea for reaching out and expressing your love for the book. Knowing that you've enjoyed this new direction means the world. I can't express how much it was needed. Thank you.

To my wonderful readers, I hope you enjoy Ellie and Owen's story and get swept away in their romance. Thank you for your continued support. Sending hugs.

DEDICATION

For H&G
To believing in Love above all else.

PROLOGUE

"Mum, leave it." I huff, dumping the remnants of my wardrobe into my suitcase.

"No, I will not leave it, Ellie. We haven't seen you in months and then you just up and leave?"

"Yes."

"Why? What's happened? If you'd just talk to me." Her arm reaches out for mine, but I bat it away, uncomfortable with her contact.

"I don't want to talk about it."

"So, there's at least something you don't want to tell me about." Her arms cross over her chest in the same disapproving way they've done ever since I was a child.

"No, Mum. Just stop." The more she pushes the faster I want to run. I knew I shouldn't have answered the door to her, but she just wouldn't stop banging on the thing.

"This isn't like you. You've been distant for months. I want to know what's going on. I'm your mother, Ellie." The words don't pierce my now armoured heart the way they would have a few months ago, and I let them roll off me like water running from my skin. I can't grow soft now. All that's been keeping me going these last few weeks is thoughts of escape.

Escape with no coming back.

I ram the last items into the case and fight the zip closed. All my other belongings have been boxed up and are already in storage. The only things I'm taking with me are the essentials.

"Ellie?"

I don't answer her and keep on task. The drive will be over five hours if I stop, and I need to get going.

"Stop, Ellie. Look at me." She grabs my arms and turns me to face her. I can't meet her eyes and stand, staring at the floor. I'm afraid that if I do, she'll see all the horrible hurt and pain in my eyes. The shame and fear I live with every day might seep from my eyes out into the world.

She stands, her hands gripping my forearms, waiting for me to speak. "What happened?" Her frustration is growing, but it doesn't change the fact that I'll never tell her, or anyone, the truth behind my decision.

The tension bubbles in the air and the lies and secrets I've kept in my head feel like a physical force standing between us.

"Tell me!" Her arms shake mine, and my body vibrates, as I stand motionless. My mind flips back in time as her hands grip tighter onto me. Fear snakes around my chest and the pain flares through my mind as if it were only yesterday.

No. No, I need to escape.

"No!" This time, I wrench my arms free from her and step away. With the distance, my mind begins to clear, and I can see the confusion etched on Mum's face.

The Ellie from six months ago would never be able to shut anyone out. She was the centre of the family, always insisting on family dinners and outings. But the switch was necessary. I had to concentrate on getting better and building my strength.

My sister, Amy, is still local to Mum and Dad, so it isn't like I'm abandoning them. I just… can't cope with staying in London, or with the constant questions and whispered comments.

"Your job, your friends. Your family? You can't just up and leave."

"I can. I need to do this. I'm sorry. Please, just let me go."

"Go where?"

"I'll be in touch." I grab the bag from the bed and walk past her into the lounge.

"Please, Ellie."

I finally meet her eyes and hope that I've been able to hide all the emotions from her that are swimming beneath the surface. "I'm sorry." I turn and walk out the door.

ONE

THREE YEARS LATER

George's tail wags a staccato beat against the bed as his impatience grows. I'm usually up by now, but all my energy fled my body this morning. My limbs feel like they've turned to marshmallow. A snuffle and grunt followed by a nudge into my neck tell me George doesn't sympathise with me. At least, not until I let him out.

As soon as I start peeling myself from the bed, George is happy. He's won.

"Okay, boy. Okay." I bundle myself in an oversized jumper and walk through to the kitchen to switch the kettle on. The back door leads down into a small garden where I let George out to do his business. With the beach on the doorstep and as much outdoor space and time as I like, not having a big garden for George to run around in isn't a problem.

"Come on. Time to get ready, George." His waggly ears prick up, and he climbs the steps back up to our first-floor apartment.

I rescued the sandy, short-haired pup shortly after I arrived in Cornwall. Packing up and moving to a place with as little crime as possible took me to the edge of the country. Literally. Remote, desolate, but wildly beautiful, I fell in love with Tregethworth the moment I drove through the little village, but it wasn't until I found George that I started to relax. And that still only happened on the rare occasion.

After making a cup of tea and feeding George, I throw on some clothes and go make camp in my office. The second bedroom of the small apartment doubles as my workspace. All I need is a desk and a computer. My clients have been slowly steady over the last few years. Not where I'd hoped to be, but enough. Just.

I jiggle the mouse, and the whir of the machine starts. While I wait, I glance at where I left my Kindle last night—still on the arm of the sofa. I take the few strides from the office to retrieve one of my favourite possessions.

Sleep crept up on me last night, and I dozed off on the sofa before I finished the chapter. It's unusual for me to fall asleep reading. In order to function the next day, I need to get at least six hours of sleep. That gives me plenty of time to read right up to midnight, but last night I couldn't keep my eyes open.

I flick the e-reader on and scan the page I abandoned last night.

Next thing I know, I've finished the next ten chapters, and I reluctantly need to answer the phone that's vibrating on my desk.

"Hello, Kerenza."

"Hi, Ellie. Just wanted to check in. Will you be popping down later? I have a file of paperwork that's just been dropped off from The Silver Tree."

"Okay, I'll be down in a bit to grab it."

"Great."

"Anything else?"

"I've cleared the emails in your account as well."

"That's great, thank you. Were there any enquiries?" I ask hopefully.

"Not today, sorry."

"No worries. See you soon." I end the call before Kez can try and convince me to do something else today. I shouldn't be so closed off—she is my only real friend in Tregethworth. Kerenza is my receptionist and assistant. I can work upstairs and keep out of the way while she handles all the contact with the clients and public.

I breathe out and look at the black screen on my desk.

An hour, and a few spreadsheets later, George follows me downstairs to the space set up as an office reception.

It was the only business property available for rent when I moved in, and it came with the apartment above. As an accountant, I don't need a shop front, but everywhere in Cornwall is a tourist spot. It's just a shame I want nothing to do with people.

She's a natural people person and didn't give me an opportunity to say no when she came in to see if I needed a hand in the first weeks I was setting up. Turns out, I'd have been lost without her. Every time the door opened, I jumped out of my skin. Hiding away in front of my computer, or better yet, with a good book on my Kindle was more my ideal, and luckily, Kez has been the buffer between the outside world and me. She's been helping me ever since, and I'm so grateful to her. She also adores George.

The door creaks open and George runs through looking for Kez.

"Oh, there's my favourite boy," she gushes as he bounds up to her at the desk. She slips from the chair and gives him a heartfelt welcome. "Alright, boy. I'll come and say hi again later, but right now I need to chat to your mum. Just curl up for a minute."

Kez smiles, grabs a box file from the desk and hands it over.

"Silvia dropped this off and said that it should all be there. I scanned through it, and most are incidental receipts. I think you already have the bulk of the info."

"Yes, that's great. I'll get this finished-off this afternoon then."

"I'll drop her an email and let her know. Is there anything else I can work on?"

"Maybe just go through the client list and check in with anything overdue to us." I smile and turn to head back upstairs.

"Can I keep George for a little while? I can take him out along the beach after work."

"Sure. Come up to get his lead when you're ready."

When I reach my apartment, I double-check the lock at the top of the stairs and then retreat into my office. The story I'm reading has already filled most of my morning, so I bury my Kindle under the box from The Silver Tree. I can finish the book as my reward for completing this set of accounts.

Two cups of tea later, I sit back in my chair feeling accomplished. I've finalised the accounts, just the covering paperwork to draw up to send off to Silvia. It's nice to see her business growing so well. Her workshop is down the road, and she makes some beautiful jewellery.

The love story I'm partway through is calling to me, so I grab my Kindle and curl up in my favourite chair by the bay window. The view across to the ocean is stunning. Many an hour has been spent watching the turn of the sea or the wrath of the weather against the shore. It's soothing, and strangely, calms a part of me that's constantly uneasy. But right now, my heart belongs to the characters that live on the pages I've immersed myself in the last day and night. The outside world can wait.

"Look into my eyes and tell me you don't feel the same. That you don't feel what's between us."

"Ellie, it's Kez!"

I drag my eyes away from the words on the screen and re-orientate myself with the help of the banging and Kez's voice.

"Coming, coming." I perch my Kindle on the windowsill and go let her in. Kez and her beautifully braided blond hair burst inside as soon as the door opens, George with her. He wags his tail triumphantly as he greets me.

"Let me guess, head in a book?" She looks up and smiles. She knows that books are my obsession, more specifically, romance books, and she indulges me. I nod to her and turn to fetch George's lead.

"Why don't you come and join me? We can take the coastal path around the headland and then come back in for a coffee?" Kez asks me out or encourages me to join her at every opportunity. It's sweet that she continues after all these years when she knows I'll only do it on a handful of occasions: when it's quiet, when I've been able to build up to the idea of venturing out, and when I have the time to calm down after.

She argues that if I can take George out for a walk or run, I should be able to go for a drink in the pub or coffee shop with her. In principle, I agree with her, but my mind doesn't work that way. My body tenses up and my nerves start, destroying any courage I'd worked up and shown to push out of my comfort zone. Plus, I have George with me. He is more than a companion—he's my security. Being a Staffordshire cross, he's as strong as he is kind. Plus, he's protective. He'd never let anything happen to me.

"Maybe tomorrow?" I answer with a small smile. She gives me the same understanding look she does every time, and I love her for it. Somehow, she knows not to push me on this subject and that I'll agree, on my terms, when I'm ready.

"You better get back to your book then. Do I need to ask what it's about?" Her eyebrows wag suggestively at me, and I sense the warmth flush over my skin.

"I think you know by now. I don't read anything other than romance."

"Well, it's nice to know some people get their happily ever after, even if they are a work of fiction." She clips George to his lead and escapes out the back door and down the steps. I walk to my window and follow Kez's figure as she makes her way down the street towards the entrance to the beach. Once they're out of sight, I curl back up and endeavour to reach my own happy ever after.

TWO

It's the final few weeks of summer and autumn is already in the air. Most people are back at work and school, turning the village quieter without the crush of families at the beach, or the constant procession through the small lanes. With the cooling temperatures, I can feel myself relax internally as the promise of quieter times comes.

The book I finished last night is still with me, and I've been invigorated by reading the character's story. Maybe I'll take Kez up on her next offer for coffee or join her on a walk.

The light creeps over the edge of the ocean and the cliffs that frame it, turning the sky a milky grey. I spot a few lone black figures on the beach ready to catch the dawn surf. George is standing patiently at my side anticipating his freedom at any moment.

"Oh, come on then. It's not going to get any quieter, is it?"

George barks, as if he understands exactly what I'm saying.

I bundle myself in my coat and scarf, even though it's barely autumn, and pull on my black boots before heading out down the back steps. George shadows me—never running more than a few feet in front as if he knows anxiety could get the better of me at any moment. I stuff my hands into my pockets and follow the path down to the beach.

The steady rumble and crash of the waves hitting the sand offer a soothing backdrop to my amble. Once on the beach, I let George run and encourage him to wear himself out.

It's beautiful. The light brightens the vista by the second, illuminating the world around us. I close my eyes and let my mind fully relax. My thoughts wander back to the trials the heroine went through in the last story I read. She was shy and reserved and felt trapped by a life she didn't want. Until she met him.

I love immersing myself in my character's worlds but can never see it happening to me. How could I ever trust a man after what happened? After what they did?

The calm that had surrounded me evaporates as the ugly pain of that night haunts me again.

"George!" I call for him, and he comes bounding over the damp sand, his doggy prints leaving a streak in his wake. I hold him to me and scan the surrounding area. Nobody is out and about. The car park only has two vehicles in it, and the surfers I viewed from my window are in the sea. I'm alone. I'm safe.

"Come on then. Time to get back in."

On the walk back home, my footsteps are hurried, and I try to block the unhappy memories from surfacing. It doesn't work. They're too potent, too horrible to fade into the background. Being ambushed as I was, has irrevocably changed my ability to be outside without taking great caution. I'd hoped it was just the raw reaction and recovery, but I still feel frightened. Panic chokes me at the thought that it could happen again.

"Hello, excuse me. My name is Alec. I'm a friend of Kez."

I jump, pulling on George's lead and turning to see who startled me to death.

"He…llo," I stutter out. My body turns to jelly, and nerves invade my limbs.

"Sorry, I didn't mean to startle you."

"Okay. But I need to get back," I utter, trying to rein in my runaway heart. My feet are purposeful against the path until I reach the safety of home. I don't look back, and a part of me cringes at how rude I've been, but I can't think about that. The man said he was friends with Kez. It shouldn't be a problem to say hello. But it is. My pulse still races as I suck in a few deep breaths. My mind is already desperate to lock myself away and banish my memories with the help of a new book. Yes, that's what I need to focus on. Unless Kez made any headway on the chase up for more clients, my work schedule is clear for a while. There's a new author that's had some great reviews online, and her debut is sitting on my Kindle ready to go.

Forbidden love. There's something about this story that just keeps my heart pounding and my finger swiping at the screen almost faster than my eyes can read the words.

Why is it that you always want something more when you can't have it? Is it just the psychology of that notion or is it deeper than that? I stir my tea, still trapped inside the book that's had me gripped all morning. I'm rooting for the heroine. She's a strong character. Loveable and sweet and mixed up in a twisted tale of love that breaks my heart. The author's words speak to me as if she wrote them just for me.

Happy ever afters are the only stories I'll read. I've suffered enough loss and pain that I need my escapism to be a fantasy world with a good ending.

I check my phone and see a message from Kez.

Coffee this afternoon? Just a quick one at Molly's x

The clouds have kept Tregethworth in constant grey all morning. I peer out of my window, and I'm pleased that there's no mass of tourists wandering up and down the roads.

Ok. I'll meet you at 3, and I'll bring George. X

:-)

Two hours. Two hours to forget about my nerves in the pages of a book.

George all but pulls me along the road and down towards the beach as we head to the coffee shop. Molly's also serves as a small general store and post office and has a large outside area for tourists to overlook the beach in the summer. Molly, the owner, has lived in Tregethworth all her life and knows everything that happens in the place. She and Kez can often be found gossiping.

The bell on the door rings as I push through, and George finds Kez sitting in one of the sofa areas in the corner of the room. My eyes cast over at all the other patrons before I make my way over to her.

"Hey, what do you fancy? Molly has a new chai spice thing on the menu."

"Um, I'll just have a hot chocolate, please."

"I'll be right back." She gives me a pointed look as if she's emphasising her words. I watch her go up to the counter and start chatting animatedly to Molly. A pang of longing hits my chest, and I wish that I could feel free enough to let go of the ball of fear that sits inside of me all the time.

George lies down at my feet and lets out a sigh big enough for the both of us. As I wait, it feels like the other few customers in the shop are all looking at me. The pressure of their stares presses in on me like a vice. It's too much to ignore, and I look up and scan the room again. No one is looking at me. The few people who are here are all busy with their own conversations. An older couple with a Labrador, a lady in her early forties perhaps, and a couple. My eyes don't meet anyone else as I take them all in.

"Hey, you alright?" Kez places the steaming mugs down on the table between us. I fight the muscles in my face to produce a smile.

"Yeah, I'm good."

"Great. So, what book have you finished this week? Now I have you out of the house, I want you to relax."

"Well, I've not finished it yet." Talking about books is

my safety net.

"So, you'll be racing back to do that tonight?"

"Maybe." My smile is natural this time, and I grin at her, thinking about the satisfaction that always comes from finishing a great book. "This story is one you really should read. It's full of angst and emotion, but all in the name of love."

"Ellie, that sounds like half the books you read."

"I know, but this one is different. The writing's more… potent somehow. More real."

"Perhaps it's time for me to dive into a book."

"Or a Kindle?"

"No. If I'm going to read, I want to hold it in my hands. What's it called?"

The door distracts me from our conversation, and I watch a man walk through to the counter. All my muscles tighten as I tense, ready to flee.

"Ellie? What's the book called?"

"Um, Two-Sided Love." My response is distracted, and she picks up on what's set my nerves off. Even George has woken up.

"Hey, it's just a guy. And a cute one, at that."

"Cute?"

"Yeah. He's tall, got a rugged look about himself. About our age."

"Kez, I'm six years older than you."

"Well, close enough. Just forget he's even here. You don't need to worry."

Her comment is exactly what I need to do. Not worry. But my body seems determined to prove both of us wrong.

I pick up my mug and sip the rich, creamy goodness. The heat scalds my tongue, and I take the distraction.

"Do you want to talk about it?" Kez asks softly. In the years that I've known her, she's only offered a handful of times. Usually in similar circumstances. Something freaks me out, and I start falling back into my state of paranoia and fear. I've never told a soul the full story, but I can't keep my reaction to being out alone, especially around men, a secret. Keeping focused helps. I run with George to clear my head and keep a grip on my sanity. Without that, you might as well just lock me up today. Every time Kez has delved, I've never gone into the details.

"Just the usual. Public places. Men. Nerves."

"And you've been here for years now. It doesn't seem to have gotten any easier for you."

"I know. It doesn't make a lot of sense." The sadness I feel coats my words.

"It doesn't have to. I understand something happened, and I don't want to pry. When you're ready, you'll share. If not, no biggie. But that guy is looking at you, and I'd like to help you not freak out about it."

"He's looking?"

"Okay, forget the guy. Tell me what the hero's like in the book. And who wrote it? If I'm going to read the thing, I want to look up the author."

"Olivia Wren is her name. It's the best book I've read all year."

"Well, that's some praise considering you've read like a gazillion."

"You exaggerate. But you really should read it."

"You don't have to keep yourself locked behind a book. There might be the right person for you out there if you'd just look." Her comment holds such sweet innocence and reminds me why I can't share my past with her. Kerenza is still so new to the world. She's barely left Tregethworth, and I don't want to taint her rosy-eyed view of the world. She doesn't need me telling her of monsters when she should be experiencing life for herself.

"Kez, I really appreciate that thought, but it's not that simple for me. Not anymore. I'm happy with my words on a page. They can't hurt you. Not like real life can."

I risk my mouth being burned again and gulp down the hot chocolate. My eyes snap up at the sensation that I'm being watched again. This time, I'm right. I look right into the stare of the guy Kez pointed out. He's the only new customer in the shop, and his table is directly facing us.

My skin heats and sweat breaks out over my palms. The prickly sensation that runs down your neck when you're scared has me reaching for George and taking hold of his lead. I look at Kez, who has a resigned look on her face. She can see I'm getting worked up and knows what's coming.

"I'm sorry, Kez. I'll be back home. Come on up if you want later, and we can finish the conversation."

"Alright. Do you want me to bring take-out?"

"Sure. Say eight?"

"The usual?"

"Yep." I pull George up, and after a quick shake, he's alert and following my lead. The man's stare feels like an arrow piercing my heart as I walk to the exit. My chest aches and my breathing quickens. As I open the door, a gust of salty wind dashes me in the face, waking me up. I shut the door and risk a glance through the glass. He's still watching me, but I see soft, gentle eyes. My brow knits into a scowl before I turn away and head back home. George leads me, pulling me along and letting my mind drift to safety.

THREE

Tears track down my face as I try to make out the words swimming in front of my eyes. My emotions for these fictional characters leak all over me, and I don't even try to hold them back. Why should I? I've been with them on a roller-coaster ride of love and heartache, willing them to find their perfect ending. The author did a wonderful job of letting me live in the safety of their fictional world.

The knock at the door doesn't give me long to digest The End, and I swipe the tears off my cheeks.

Kez is standing at the top of the steps with a bag of Chinese food. "Hey, sorry, I lost track of the time."

"Is that the book? Did you finish it?"

"Yes."

"And? You've been crying, and I want to make sure they're happy tears from the story rather than anything else," she asks as she puts the bag on the counter before moving to grab two plates from the cupboard.

"It's all good. They have a perfect ending and are starting the rest of their lives together."

"Great. Well, there are two things I need to talk to you about. Good news or bad. What do you want first?"

"Bad?" I ask, not sure what she's going to come out with.

"Okay. Well. You know I consider you a friend as well as my boss."

"Yes, of course. And I the same, although not the boss part, the assistant."

"Good. Because I think you really need to look at your business. We have all this space downstairs, and it's a complete waste. You could be utilising it to obtain a second income. It would help." She looks like she's not sure if she's said too much. As soon as the words fly from her mouth, she begins nibbling her finger.

The proposition is interesting, though terrifying. "What did you have in mind?" She wouldn't have brought this up without a plan. Kez is thorough.

"I have a friend, who's an amazing photographer. His work would totally sell here. He can show his photos, and you can charge rent. A gallery space that I can run as well as the accountant stuff." She looks eager and excited. "You need to do something. Your accounts are a ticking time bomb. You need to do something."

Her announcement coupled with a beaming smile has me caught between my own variety of excitement and anxiety. I'd have more people to deal with. Or the potential for people. My reaction is instantaneous, and my heart jumps. Kez can read my reaction without me saying a word.

"Relax. I can deal with the public. You'd just need to have a conversation with Alec to set up the…"

"Alec? I think he tried to talk to me on the beach. He said he was a friend of yours, but I pretty much walked right off and ignored him."

"Honestly, he's a softy. He won't hold it against you. I wouldn't suggest it if I didn't know him. I know you can do it."

My heart stutters in my chest, but as its beats get faster, I can see the business needs help. Kez is right.

"You think he'd go for it?"

"Absolutely. It would be perfect." Her enthusiasm gushes. "Just one meeting. Get things rolling."

"Ok. Fine." I can do that.

"He's harmless. I promise. You can't be behind the scenes all the time. I say this as your friend; you need to meet your clients more. That's why you're not doing as well as you should. You hide away, Ellie."

"I know. There's a reason for that. Besides, if I didn't, I wouldn't need you to work for me. So how about we think of something else." My tone is harsher than I wanted. Kez is doing this out of kindness and concern. She deserves more. "I'm sorry," I huff out.

"Look, I can meet Alec with you, but this is your business. Okay?" She smiles. "Oh, and we have a new client."

"You couldn't have led with that?"

"No, I couldn't. And it's not confirmed. I mean, you have a new enquiry, so fingers crossed." The smile she was sporting a moment ago now beams off her face. She's practically bouncing off the chair.

"That's great." I smile at her, not really understanding

why a new customer would get her all worked up like this.

"It is. Wait until you hear who." She pulls her attention to dishing up our favourite indulgent food—Chinese takeout—before taking the plates to the small kitchen table.

The smell of ginger and spices is comforting, even if we both know it's not the healthiest of food choices. It's our one vice, and something we've bonded over.

"Okay, Kez. Am I going to have to check the emails myself, or will you spill the beans?"

"Well, I went back to the shop after coffee and was chasing up a few things when you got an email enquiry. The name seemed familiar, and after I did a little google searching, I realised it's the author you just read. Olivia Wren."

Her comment stops me dead. My heart thumps wildly in my chest, and the nerves that spring up are welcome because for once they are excited nerves rather than the terrifying, turn you to stone and make you feel sick, kind.

"Are you sure? Could it just be a coincidence?" First a new business venture, and now the possibility to work with an author I've read. I'm all over the place.

"No, I did the first email response to check to see if they might be a time waster—you know, looking at the accounts for a free pointer—and she confirmed that she's a writer who recently moved to the area. She hasn't set up her accounts before and wants to make sure she gets on top of everything."

Kez's words sink in, and I realise they match with what I've heard. Olivia Wren is somewhat of a new author. Could it be she really *is* in the area and needs some help? The fork of lemon chicken is forgotten as I internally stop to process my excitement.

The little smile that Kez gives has me hardening my expression.

"Oh, why did you do that? It's not often I get to see an excited Ellie. Hell, I can't remember when you've ever been excited before. It's nice."

"Kez, this woman…" I start but stop and try to work out how to explain just what a big deal it is that an author who I've read and loved could be working with me. "Her words are phenomenal. She writes like no one else I know, and believe me, I've read a lot of romance books. The style is different. More visceral. Please tell me you'll read it now?"

"Yes, yes, of course. But does that mean we'll take her on as a client?"

"Of course." I beam. "What did you say in the last email?"

"Just that I'll be in touch." She pastes a sheepish look on her face. "And what about Alec?"

Her suggestion was sound and my business brain that's been slumbering for the last few years knew it could be an excellent idea. Making ends meet wasn't always easy, and I didn't like dipping into my savings. "Fine. Will you contact him? He'll have to come here. To meet, that is."

"Sure. I'll get back to Olivia as well."

"Wait! I want to do that. It's an email, right?" I look up from the food and realise I've spoken out loud. My heart judders at the thought of having direct contact with a stranger, but Olivia doesn't feel like a stranger. She feels like a friend. What harm can it do, being on the end of a computer screen?

"Wow, okay, that's a first."

"Do you mind?" It's a ridiculous thing to say, but Kez has handled all my clients since day one. I don't want to offend her, but there's an excitement about this possibility that's overtaking me.

"Of course not." Kez pulls a face at me as if I'm being stupid.

"Okay." I relax back in my chair and contemplate everything that's gone through my mind tonight. For me, this is a huge step and something completely out of my comfort zone. Since moving here, I've avoided contact with people beyond anything that's necessary. I've become a ghost of the woman I once was, hiding away in the worlds I read, rather than embracing what's on my doorstep.

But for me, I can't bring myself to find that freedom to trust in anyone that's around me. It's too big a step and one that I'm not ready to take.

We retreat into comfortable silence, happy to devour the food in front of us, while my mind forces the memories of that terrible day from invading. They always do. They are as much a part of me as my arm or my love of reading. Escaping them is never going to be something I can achieve, but I've started to control my reactions to them. My waking memories, at least.

"So, will you set up a meeting?" Kez asks around a mouthful of noodles.

"Let's not rush things, Kez. Maybe. But I'd like to send her an email first."

"Okay, well keep me posted. Come on, there's a film

I want to watch." She picks up her plate, carries it through into the front room and curls up on the sofa. I hand her the remote and take my usual seat by the window.

For once, the film isn't some soppy romance. With all the books about love I read, I should be a regular chick-flick viewer, but I can't stand that they only hold a tenth of the power a book does. Give me a mystery or a thriller, and I'll at least pay attention.

"Right, that's it for me tonight." George lifts his head from his bed as Kez moves to leave.

I say goodbye to Kez and let George out before I lock up for the night.

As I lie in bed, I'm wide-awake, but I don't want to reach for a new book. My mind is still fluttering over what I should say to Olivia.

It's useless. I grab my phone and pull up the work email account. Sure enough, there's an email from Olivia Wren in the folder. I tap the screen and see a perfectly normal email asking for accountancy services.

Dear Olivia,

Thanks for reaching out. I'd be happy to help. Kerenza says that you're an author and you've recently moved to the area. It's a lovely part of the world.

Have you registered with HMRC as yet?

Ellie Carter

I put the phone down and stare at the ceiling. My body is full of triumph at such a stupidly little milestone, but for me, it's a milestone that is a huge step. And it's all because this particular woman wrote the most fantastic book.

My phone chimes and my eyes spring open as I grab my phone.

Dear Ellie,
Thank you for getting back to me personally. Yes, I've registered with HMRC, and I've received a letter asking me to submit a tax return. Hence the enquiry. It's rather late to be emailing clients, isn't it?
Olivia

My face splits into a wide grin at her last comment.

Hi Olivia,
Well, I don't always keep strict business hours.
Can you send me a copy of the letter? I'll need to request authorisation to handle your tax affairs. Have you kept copies of all your sales invoices and expenses?
Thanks,
Ellie

This time, I keep hold of my phone, hoping she'll reply again. I feel like a silly teenager waiting to catch a glimpse of their idol. It's crazy, but the most fun I've had for a while. That thought depresses me and stops me in my tracks. How have I let myself remain the victim? Wasn't it enough that they took my life from me, ruined me for anyone else and barely let me escape with my life? I've allowed myself to live in such fear that a simple email exchange has been the most spontaneous thing I've done in years.

Ellie,

I'm a bit of a night owl myself. Luckily, working for myself and doing what I do, offers a certain amount of flexibility when it comes to my working pattern.

Olivia

Olivia,

Well, even for you writers, your productivity must wane given the hour. Send me the documents when you can, and we can get started. Looking forward to working with you.

Ellie

FOUR

I wait eagerly for another email from Olivia, but there's radio silence for the next few days. My high from that first exchange has tumbled back to my usual reality, but one thing that has stuck with me is how insular and scared I've become.

I was brave enough to move across the country and start again on my own. How is it that going for a coffee with my best friend is such a concern?

Since Friday, I've had a determination within me to try harder. To learn to relax and not see everyone I meet as a potential assailant. In my narrow world, that means initiating going for coffee with Kez. We had to talk about meeting her photographer friend. The more I gave the idea thought, the more sense it made, and I couldn't ignore it. The business needed an injection of clients, and if they weren't in abundance, I had no choice. Not if I wanted to ensure I could keep Kerenza employed through another winter.

"Are you feeling alright? I mean, of course I'll meet you for a coffee."

"Thanks. I've done quite a lot of thinking since the other night."

"Great. Shall I meet you there in say, half an hour?"

"Sure." I end the call and breathe through my automatic response to clam up and feel pressure growing over my body.

"George, you'll look out for me, won't you?" His woof of confirmation beats back the panic, and I power through the motions of getting ready.

Half an hour later, I'm sitting in the coffee shop, my feet bouncing on the floor as I wait nervously for Kez to show. I've only looked around the shop once. It was instinctual when I entered—assessing the danger and whether I was brave enough to go in—but apart from that, I have resisted. George has made his home next to my feet, and it's his presence that's keeping me on an even keel right now.

The vibration of my phone in my bag makes me jump. I dig it out and quickly see a new email.

Ellie,

Sorry it's taken me a few days to come back to you, I've been buried in words. Here's the form attached and the details you requested. I have a stack of papers that I'm sure will all need to come to you. How about we meet for a coffee, and I can hand them over? Sorry, they're not all electronic.

Olivia

Meet?

I lock the phone without replying. That familiar feeling of excitement mixed with trepidation fuels my blood, and it goes straight to my head. The nervous, sick feeling invades my stomach as I foresee holding a conversation with a stranger. Sometimes it's hard with Kez, and she already knows and understands my awkwardness and that there will be periods of silence where I'm struggling to find the words to fill and would rather be locked in my own head.

But that's not the person I want to be. I'm trying to find strength and fighting to be the person I was—outgoing and lively. I look around the shop, hoping to see Kez. She's running a few minutes late, which isn't like her.

As I cast my eyes around, I try and picture myself here, but with Olivia Wren sitting opposite. What would I say to her? Should I tell her I've read her book and that it was the best I've come across in a long time? Would that make it awkward?

"Sorry, I'm sorry. Alec called me as I was on my way down and he wouldn't get off the phone." Kez bundles her way into the seat next to me, waking George who clearly doesn't mind as he gets an affectionate scratch behind the ears as an 'I'm sorry'.

"That's fine." I grab for my mug of coffee and wait for Kez to launch into whatever questions of conversation topic she might have.

"So, thank you for calling."

"It's fine. We saw each other Friday night."

"Yes, but this is the first time you've asked me to go out. In three years. It's brilliant. And I mentioned to Alec that I spoke to you about his photos." She beams, happy about my small victory.

"What did he say?"

"Ellie, this is something you need to do. It's your business. I'll be there with you at the meeting, but you need to instigate it. Alec is from Tregethworth as well. He's nice. I promise he's nothing to be frightened of."

"It's easier said than done, Kez." She was right though. If I were to expand the business, it needed to come from me.

"Can you ask him to come to the shop tomorrow maybe?" I wish I sounded surer of myself. But then I think about my conversation with Olivia. And that she wants to meet. Maybe meeting Alec could be practice.

Kez rubs a hand over mine, belying her age, her maturity suddenly shining through.

"Olivia Wren wants to meet," I mutter. Perhaps if I say it quietly, it won't seem such a huge deal to my brain.

"That's great, and not entirely unexpected. I usually meet most of the clients. They come into the office to drop off the paperwork, sign the final reports, that sort of thing. It's just something you've never wanted to handle."

"I know. And I still don't. But this is Olivia. She's like a famous movie star to me, and I've got the chance to have coffee with her. What would I say? I don't want to be awkward around her."

"You're not awkward. You just sometimes prefer to live inside the pages of your book or inside your head, rather than with the person in front of you. I still love you. And this is good. An opportunity."

"Thank you." Kez is one-hundred-percent right, and I can't thank her enough for tolerating my idiosyncrasies.

My eyes skip across the room and land on a man who I think I recognise from the last time we were here. He looks… normal. He has brown, messy hair, but in a trendy way. A brush of light stubble covers his chin, and I scan up to warm eyes. He's watching me, and my body reacts. I can feel my muscles tensing up, ready to deploy my flight reflex at this sign of danger.

"Don't run, Ellie." I hear her implore as I sit frozen in place.

Her words sink in, and I bend down to give George an affectionate rub. He won't let anything happen to me, and I want to stop feeling like the victim. How am I meant to get through a potential business meeting if I can't cope with being in the same shop as a guy?

"I'm not."

"Good. So, are you going to meet up with Olivia?"

"Will you come as well? You know, like you are with Alec?" It's an obvious solution and one that won't be too suspicious. Kerenza is my assistant.

"Um, sure. If you really need to bring me along. I doubt I'll have finished the book before the meeting though. I'm still waiting for the delivery."

"I've told you that a Kindle is the way to go."

"And I've told you I love a real book when I read."

We both giggle and the tension ebbs away. It feels good to be doing something so normal, like a jigsaw piece that doesn't quite fit into place until you try it around the right way.

The door closes, and I watch the man walk past the front window with a takeaway cup in hand. He smiles at me watching him, but instead of returning his grin, I turn away before the blush that heats my cheeks is visible and busy myself with my own coffee like someone who just got caught looking at something she shouldn't.

"Why don't you set a meeting with Olivia before you get cold feet?" Kez brings my attention back to the room.

I nod.

Olivia,
A meeting would be great. I can introduce you to my assistant as well. Do you know Molly's next to the beach? When would be convenient?
Ellie

Short and to the point. I hold the phone in my hand waiting for the reply to pop up, but it doesn't. Of course, she could be busy or not at her computer. I shouldn't assume that she spends every minute at her screen typing the next words ready for me to read.

"Did you want me to walk you back?"

"Huh?"

"Home? Unless you want to stay longer?"

"Oh, I was going to take George for a walk on the beach as it's low tide. You're welcome to join me?"

"I should get back to the shop, really. Although I'll happily take him off your hands another day this week?"

"Anytime." We both get up to leave, and I force air into my lungs and back out again, much like I force my steps to look calm and relaxed, rather than strained and nervous.

An hour or so later with a wet dog in tow, we make it back to the house. George goes to curl up in his bed, and I flick the switch to boil the kettle and put the computer on.

I bring up my inbox, hopeful that I can set the meeting up with Olivia sooner rather than later as I attempt to get over the anxiety that surrounds it.

Ellie,
Yes, I know Molly's. I was there earlier today. It's funny how we haven't bumped into each other before. I'll be back in the village on Thursday if that suits you? I have a file of paperwork with your name on it.
Looking forward to talking in person.
Olivia

Three days.

I have three days to work up the courage to hold a proper conversation with someone other than the few people that are now in my life.

Olivia,
Yes, I was also there earlier. We must have just missed each other. Would Thursday at 10 a.m. suit? And don't worry, we have plenty of time to organise the paperwork. Kerenza and I will look forward to seeing you on Thursday.
I must admit, I've read your last book, so I'm especially excited to meet you in person.
Ellie

Ellie,

Okay, well that changes things a bit. Meeting my readers is a step further than I've been comfortable with so far. I guess I can start with you, Ellie. Do I dare ask your opinion on my book?

O

I stare at the screen for a moment, contemplating my response. Should I write a response? I don't need to, but there's a part of me that longs for a connection to someone, and to work towards building a trust that I've been too frightened to even start with for all this time.

The screen goes black and into sleep mode before I make up my mind, and I have to re-boil the kettle as it's taken so long to get around to making tea.

10 a.m. at Molly's on Thursday. You okay to meet Olivia Wren then?

I text Kez and go back to pondering a response to Olivia.

Olivia,

It was amazing. That doesn't sound enough to describe how good the book was. Sorry, I'm better with numbers than words. Reading is my thing, not writing.

Ellie

Ellie,

I'll settle for amazing. Does this mean the meeting

is on now I know you don't hate the story?
    O

My smile is genuine as I look over the exchange. Before throwing my phone down, I flick to the photos on my phone, nostalgia making an appearance and running rife through me. My finger swipes past the dozens and dozens of pictures of the Cornish landscape in its various seasons. A few photos of the shop and the odd one of Kez or George is all that's on there from the last three years.

You can see the change instantly as if someone put a bookmark on the date that it happened. There are hundreds of photos *before*, all with friends, family and other random shots I wanted to capture. There are selfies with a woman who's smiling, her blond curly hair bouncing and as full of life as she looks. My curls are more of a mess now. I haven't looked after my hair for years—what's the point? Why would I do anything that would make me look attractive? I pull my hair from the band and see if one of the corkscrew-curls will do anything other than hang limply from my head.

No bounce.

The faces that I see smiling back at me were my friends and co-workers. Those who helped me build a successful and fun-filled life.

I throw the phone onto the desk and pull up a Google search for a hairdresser in the area. There's one just outside of Tregethworth which is open late on Mondays. They only list women on their staff.

Perfect.

FIVE

"What… look at you, you look amazing!" I open the door to Kez, and she blasts in, surrounding me and fussing as if she's not seen me in months. "You've got the most amazing hair, and I've only just seen this. How come?" She comes up and pings one of my ringlets.

"Hey," I protest, hating that people still do that.

"You can't show me this gorgeous hair and not expect me to want to ping it."

"I can. The hair isn't for touching. And it will calm down tomorrow. It was a rash decision and one that terrified me for every second I was there, but it was long overdue."

"I'm so proud of you. I don't know if this is all because you're having a meeting with that author, but it's great to see." Kez engulfs me in a hug, and I suddenly seem like the younger of the two of us, wrapped up in her praise and acceptance.

"Thank you." The words stick in my throat, suddenly caught by the emotion that bubbles up like a fizzy drink waiting to be opened.

"Are you ready?"

"Yes, sure." I lie.

She smiles and then heads back down the internal staircase to the door of the shop.

As I look around the room, there's plenty of space to utilise for photographs on the wall. We can even put in a sofa or seating to make it inviting. Before the attack, I'd have seen the opportunity myself and snatched it. Now, it's been up to Kez to fight for my business.

Alec is older than both of us. Mid-to-late thirties. He carries a black case as he enters.

"Hi, Ellie." He walks up to meet with his hand extended. It causes me to draw breath, but I force myself to move the muscles in my arm and offer my hand in return. Kez is right next to me.

"Alec. Kez has told me lots about you." The words stick in my mouth and come out without too much force.

"Would you like to see some of my work?"

I take a seat at the desk where Kez usually works, and he places the black folder in front of me. I flip open the cover and see a vibrant splash of oranges and golds. A dark and craggy outcrop of rocks creates the contrast to the colour.

As I flick through, I see the landscape that's around us displayed in beautiful shots. Colours that I thought impossible, bleed off the page in his photographs. "These are amazing." It's an honest reaction.

"Thank you." Pride warms his voice.

Kez jumps in, much to my relief. "We thought the space could double as a gallery with your pieces on the wall. I can run the shop but would expect you to be able to pop in and talk with customers if you're free. There would be a low, standard rent, with a commission on sales." She runs off the outline but stops short. Her eyes grow huge in her face as she realises she's taken over. I grin and raise my eyebrows, giving her the okay to continue. My hands in my lap are damp with sweat as I wait for Alec to say anything further or ask me a direct question.

"Any questions?" Kez looks around us all.

"Um, no. I'd like to set up some internal hanging and lighting to display the work. I'm happy to invest if the rent and commission are right and if this can be a permanent arrangement."

"Six-month trial," I pipe up. I don't want to be locked into anything that doesn't work. My heart pumps against my rib cage.

"Sorry, Ellie, but it's the start of the winter season. We need to evaluate this through the summer before we know if it will work." Alec holds my eyes, and it sends every part of me into panic mode. It's not an option right now. I'm determined to overcome this. My teeth grind together. He has a point. "A year. We can review after that." The words come out rushed as I take a gasp of air.

Alec nods, and I rip my eyes back to his photographs the moment I can.

"This is so exciting." Kez claps her hands together in joy.

"Thank you." Alec indicates to his folder, which I close and pass back to him. "I better start getting organised. Kez, I'll be in later to measure up?"

"Sure."

Alec nearly rushes from the shop, leaving Kez and me alone.

"Hey, that was good. Well done. I'm proud of you."

It's ridiculous. I need to do this to help secure my business and future, and I struggled. It's a wakeup call that I need but find impossibly difficult.

Kez must sense my mind has taken a tangent. "What have you got on for today? I'm happy to take George out for you? Or I can open up and leave you to it."

"I'll probably take him down to the beach. The weather looks pretty wet and grey, so it will be safe enough." Kez discards my words as the norm, but I see the change in her face as she takes them in.

"Don't say that. You were so good with Alec. You can do this, Ellie."

I turn away and walk over to fetch George's lead.

"I've got some initial paperwork to file for Olivia's account when I get back."

"Don't do that. Don't shut yourself off. I want to help. You've just taken such a big step." It's the first time that Kez has pushed…

"I'm sorry. It's better this way."

"For whom? I think if you've got the courage to up sticks and move, to escape whatever it was that happened to you, then you should have the courage to learn to live your life again. You can fight again, Ellie. I know it. And I'll help. Whatever I can do."

I drop my head and breathe in to try and calm my racing heart. I know she means well, but I've never let the story slip past my lips. How could I? Admitting all the foul and dirty things they subjected me to—I wouldn't be able to live with the pity in her eyes whenever she looked at me. Isolated and introspective I can cope with. Victim—not so much.

"Just understand that it's something I can't talk about. It's in the past, and that's where it needs to stay. Excuse me."

George follows as I make a beeline for the front door, and I walk out into the grey drizzle before Kez can push anymore. He runs ahead of me, bounding around towards the small garden before I catch up and clip his lead on.

The soft dust-like particles of moisture hang in the air, coating my face and clothing and soaking me within moments, but I don't care. The salty air infuses my body and sets to calm my fraying nerves.

It isn't Kez's fault. She's only trying to help me, and all I do is keep her at a distance. But the way the nurses looked at me, with such pity as they nursed me back to health—I couldn't see that from Kez. It's better she doesn't know. It's better than no one knows.

The beach is nearly deserted, and I let George loose. He runs off, before realising he needs to stay with me for protection and tears back the way he came. His fuss fills my heart, and I encourage him to run. He doesn't go far, and his constant checking is the reassurance I've come to rely on when out for walks and runs. His companionship has been a constant. One that I'm happy and grateful for.

I lose myself in my head, pretending that I might live inside the pages of the books I read. The possibility of a love so intense it burns everything else to the ground is an appealing fantasy for someone who's never been in love. The wonder and excitement are something I can almost taste.

Of course, there's no way I'll ever be able to feel that magic if I stay locked inside my own head. I survey the surrounding area. A handful of people wander the beach; surfers chase the waves to shore. There's no real threat. Molly's sits on the corner of the beach, a few people outside on the tables despite the fine drizzle.

My feet turn me in the direction of the little coffee shop, and George trots along beside me. Without my usual surveillance of the inside, I push the door open, and a welcoming blanket of warmth, along with the aroma of coffee and chocolate meets me. I keep my eyes on the counter and walk up to order a takeaway cup.

"Hi, I'll have a caramel latte please, to take away."

"Coming up, Ellie."

I smile at Molly. I still haven't looked to see who else might be in the shop and my heart is begging me to, hammering on my chest as a reminder.

"Hi." The voice is deep and sounds so close to my ear. I can't hide my automatic reaction to start and turn to the sound of his voice.

The guy. The same one from the previous few times I've visited is standing next to me, waiting to order.

"Takeaway? You're usually a drink-in type." His observation sends me flying into a panic. He must be able to see it cross my features as he starts to back up and retract his words right away. "No, no, sorry. That sounded wrong. I just meant I've seen you in here a couple of times now. I'm usually the takeaway." He smiles, and it turns his face into a stunning vision—handsome and filled with warmth—but the other side of my brain crushes that information and taints any pleasant thought or feeling with one of pain and anguish.

The second my coffee hits the counter I grab it and turn to leave the shop.

"I'm sorry, I really didn't mean to offend. Here, let me get that." He holds open the door for me to escape, George quick on my heels. "I'm Owen, by the way."

"Ellie," I whisper. I don't know why I feel the need to reply, but for some reason, I want to give him my name. I don't stop to chat though, and I head back up the street before Owen has the opportunity to talk to me anymore.

Once I've shut the door behind me and towelled off George, I try and get my head around my accomplishment. Of course, for many, giving your name to someone isn't any kind of accomplishment. And, at the time, I was trying to leave. But I was able to stop and see him. Actually let my eyes run his body and connect to his, watch the smile he gave me before I turned to run.

SIX

I mull over our encounter for the next few days until Thursday and the meeting with Olivia. What with Alec moving into the shop and meeting Owen, I have enough distractions that my nerves at meeting an actual author I've read have slipped away. Until today.

Kez is meeting me downstairs, so I grab my bag and make sure my notebook is in there before taking George down the internal stairs into the shop.

Alec is chatting with Kez, and the room quietens as I walk in.

"Hey, you ready?" she calls to me. My body freezes as I see Alec. But he's going to be around a lot. Turning into a living statue whenever he's around isn't going to work.

"Yep. Shall we go?" I fidget with my bag and check I have my keys and phone.

I take George out and let Kez follow. Alec slips behind the desk after Kez, and she bounces from the shop.

"You don't mind Alec staying, do you?"

"There's nothing of value in the shop that isn't his."

She smiles at me before changing the subject. "I'm

excited. Are you?" Her grin stretches from ear to ear, and it's infectious.

"A little. More nervous than excited." It seems it's been a week of firsts.

"Come on then." She takes my arm in hers and starts to lead us to Molly's.

"I spoke to a guy the other day." My confession is enough to stop Kez in her tracks.

"Excuse me? What? When? Who? Tell me the who first."

"It's the guy from Molly's. He's been in there every time I've been in lately. He spoke to me at the counter. I tried to run away, but I ended up giving him my name." I cringe at how awful that sounds.

"That's good. I mean, it's sort of good. It's an improvement for you, anyway."

My stomach cartwheels inside me as I get closer and closer to the shop. I imagine what the *before* Ellie would be like, meeting a woman she admires. *I can do this. I can.*

Kez walks in first and heads right up to the counter. It's busy, which is unusual, and it immediately throws off all the confidence I've been trying to build. A large group of people are congregated around the counter and spilling out into the seating area. I've never seen Olivia and have no idea what she looks like, but I still scan the room looking for anyone on their own.

"Hi, you know, I really don't have a caffeine habit, I promise." Owen is standing in front of me. My feet stutter backwards, and although there's nothing threatening about him, I can't shake the automatic reaction I have around men.

"Sorry, sorry." He backs off and takes a step away, giving me plenty of space.

I shake my head, unable to twist my tongue around the words I want to say.

"Look, I think I should be honest. I'm here to meet someone…"

"I'm sorry, Owen. Excuse me." I ease past him and look for Kez in the muddle of tourists all grabbing a takeaway drink. A pang of guilt hits my stomach and mixes with the other anxiety and excitement that has set up home.

My body tenses as I move through the people. I bump into a couple and start to feel claustrophobic around so many bodies. Each touch pushes the memories to the surface of my mind and raises my heartbeat. My breathing quickens as I fight to draw breath.

"Ellie, I just, it would be really great if you could hear me out?" Owen follows me through the mass of people.

"Owen, I'm here to meet someone. Maybe next time." If I didn't sound like a bitch before, I certainly do now, but my manners are the last thing I need to worry about. Panic starts to claw up my throat, and the room constricts in on me. My fight or flight flicks into action and pushes a burst of adrenaline through my blood. I turn away and lead George back towards the door, hurrying to free myself. The hum of the room drowns out my pounding heart, but I feel it vibrating inside me. I fly out of the door and breathe in the air.

Escape.

That's what I feel when I take the salty air into my lungs. My phone vibrates in my pocket, and I hope it might be

Olivia. It's not.

Where are you? Kez

Rain check. I'll explain later.

I look back and see a confused Kez standing to the side of the horde. Owen lingers at a table in the far corner, but I can't feel guilty about him. With my excitement in ruins and my panic attack under control, I stride out over the sand and let George free.

Dear Olivia,
I'm very sorry I wasn't able to meet you today. Honestly, I have some anxiety issues, and they got the better of me today. I'm sorry if I caused you a needless trip. I'd hate to think I pulled you away from your writing.
Ellie

Dear Ellie,
No apologies. A trip to get some air has done me good. I can't work all hours of the day. I'm sorry to hear you suffer from anxiety. I can only imagine how that might affect you. Would meeting in a different location help?
O

I find it easy opening up over email. It's like I'm writing my own story. I can live it through words rather than experience it first-hand, and it gives me the confidence to say what I genuinely feel.

Dear Olivia,
It's something I'm working on. I have good days and bad days. It's why I first started reading. Small steps.
Molly's is fine, really.
Ellie

You haven't always read?
O

No. Books have been a type of salvation for me. I bought my Kindle about three years ago. Since then I've devoured anything with a romance storyline.
They allow me to experience life in a non-threatening way. To daydream and hope for better, all from the comfort of my home.
How did you get into writing? Have you always wanted to be an author?
Ellie

My question has me sitting up, eager to see what Olivia says. If you'd have told me a week ago that I would be having a conversation with one of my current favourite authors, I wouldn't have believed you, yet, I have the email thread to prove it.

Writing wasn't something I anticipated doing with

my life. Honestly, I can't explain why I started. It was something I was drawn to. It gave me hope. And I've had a blast. And this book seems to have been a success compared to my previous titles. You'll see when you get the paperwork.

O

Other titles? I couldn't find any under your author name online? Have you written more? I'd love to give them a try.

Ellie

I wait for the email to come back and give me the titles to go and stalk, but it doesn't come. The balloon of excitement that had been filling inside of me deflates and leaves me feeling like I've been missing… something, for quite some time.

A connection. A spark. An automatic interest to talk to someone with the same interests and passions. Kez is my only friend, but she only tolerates my enthusiasm over stories. She doesn't live them the same way as I do.

Perhaps I need to change that and build on the small steps I've taken to grow the number of people in my life whom I can call a friend—put my trust in.

SEVEN

The soft wrap of knuckles on the door can mean only one thing—Kez is visiting. I reluctantly put down my Kindle and pull a warm, fleece-lined jacket around my body before answering the door.

"Morning." She's all bright and breezy like she is all the time. You can't help but feel the need to smile in her presence because she doesn't give you the option not to. "Here." She pushes a large lever arch file into my arms before trotting into the kitchen to fetch coffee.

"What's this?" I peek open the folder and see a number of printed receipts.

"It was dropped off first thing this morning by a courier. Sorry, I opened it just like I do all of your business mail. I brought it up right away."

I place the folder on my desk and open it up fully. Olivia Wren's details are over the first few pages, together with some meticulous filing of expenditure and printouts. All that I'd need to start on her accounts except the HMRC information.

The new sense of hope shrivels up inside my chest. An

opportunity—the first opportunity I've been excited about going after in years has passed me by because I was too scared, too stupid to take a small leap of faith.

"Hey, what's wrong?" Kez comes over and hands me a steaming mug of coffee.

"Oh, it doesn't matter. It's just… for the first time in forever, I felt like I wanted to try and reach out and meet this woman. I thought I was happy with how I'd built my life, but I can't deny how disappointed I am. Perhaps something needs to change?" My shoulders sink with my admission. Growing strong enough to be out around people again wouldn't be a simple errand.

"That's fantastic," Kez chirps. I look up at her, confused that she sees this as a good thing.

"And how do you work that out?" I ask, once again astounded at her optimism.

"You've felt disappointment, and we can turn that into a motivation to get you back out there. You clearly want to meet this author. Don't let this stop you. What about having a drink. You can talk business or stray into books. Whatever you're comfortable with."

"I'm not sure." My confidence has taken a knock, but there's still that echo inside of me that's desperate for me to step up and make this happen. I've met with Alec and moved forward with the business. A drink with Olivia should be possible.

"What's the harm? I promise. Nothing will happen if you're meeting at Molly's. You need to start grasping life while you can." Kez's eyes look sad as she delivers her version of tough love.

"I'll invite her to coffee."

"And my work here is done. I'll be back downstairs. Is there anything you need me to look at?"

"We probably need to look at the arrangement for Alec. I haven't the money to invest in a lot of signage or anything like that. But perhaps we could start some social media work? Now the season's over it will be hard to establish a small gallery without tourists. Is that what we're calling it, a gallery?"

"Studio, gallery. Either. And I'm on it. He's bringing in some new work as well."

I nod. This would be good for Kez as well. "Great. I trust your judgement. If you can, take a look and see what we need to do?"

"I'll let you know."

Dear Olivia,

Thank you for the paperwork. All received, and I can start work today. I'm still missing the HMRC info though. I'm sorry you felt the need to send it directly. I'd still like to meet if you want. Molly's? I promise to be there this time.

Ellie

I sit back in my chair and wait. My inbox remains quiet, and so I pick up the file of papers and begin to scan through them. Of course, as soon as I do, I hear the faint ping of a new message.

Ellie,

I'm glad you received them. I wanted to make things easy for you. I'd be more than happy to meet, but only if you're sure. I enjoy our email conversations and am happy to continue these until you feel more comfortable. After all, you don't know me.

O

Olivia,

No, please, I'd like to meet. It's what I need to do. Besides, I'd really like to talk about your book and what you're writing next. And I do feel like I know you. Or at least, I don't consider you a stranger.

Ellie

Ellie,

Well, I'm pleased about that. And I feel the same. What are the chances of finding an accountant in Tregethworth who also has read my work? It was meant to be.

O

Olivia,

It's a small world. I'm looking forward to meeting you in person. Really. Are you free at ten tomorrow morning?

Ellie

My heart is in my mouth as I press send.

Ellie,
Tomorrow it is. 10 a.m.
O

The words of the book I'm currently reading don't help to whisk me off and forget about the feeling of foreboding knotting in my stomach. Nerves wreck me all night, as I know that I'll have nowhere to hide tomorrow. Stupid. When I'm emailing, there's none of that.

I hold my head high as I walk through the door of Molly's. There's no crowd today to intimidate or obscure the small shop. I've arrived a little early, purposefully, and order a coffee. The slight tremble in my hand tells me that I need to do a better job of calming. It's just a drink. The words speed through my mind on repeat, forcing my brain to concentrate on something other than this meeting.

I take the hot caffeine hit over to the window seats and sink down into the armchair.

"Hi, would you mind?" Owen has his hand on the chair as I look up at him.

"Um, well… it's…" He slides into the seat before I can finish the words.

"I wanted to apologise for the other day. I didn't mean to startle you or cause you to leave."

"No, it's fine." I grab the mug and warm my hands around it. "I'm actually meeting someone now." My words aren't as confident as I'd hoped, but this is the longest conversation I've had with a stranger for years. It doesn't prevent me from keeping my eyes on my surroundings. Not least because I'm hoping Olivia will arrive, and I can start to concentrate on her rather than my surroundings. I scan the area and hope that Owen can take the hint.

"I know." His words send alarm bells screaming inside my head. How does he know I'm waiting for someone? "Before you up and leave again, please let me explain." He shifts in his seat, trying to settle himself. He's not full of bravado or arrogance, and I feel the first rope of tension lessen inside of me. "My name is Owen Riggs, but you may know me under another guise. Olivia Wren."

The words echo loudly in my skull like he's just signalled a warning bell, and the reverberations ripple through me. My heart stops in my chest, unprepared to comprehend what he's just told me. *How? What?*

He gives me a shy smile "I'm sorry I didn't tell you the truth. But I realised after the first couple of times I bumped into you that this might be a big deal for you. After the last meeting attempt, I thought keeping the conversation to email would help."

No no no. My mind begins to spiral out of control, but one thing sticks with me: the words on the pages of Two-Sided Love. Olivia's book.

"You wrote Two-Sided Love?" A nasty wave of betrayal smashes into me at the realisation I've been tricked. *Deceived.*

My life is a shell of how I used to live thanks to the devious and cruel nature of men. And now it's encroached on the one lifeline I believed I had. The written word has the power to give me back some of that life, to experience love and friendship and all the other beautiful emotions that a writer pours onto the page.

Writers like Olivia Wren.

Owen Riggs.

"I did." His reply is soft, almost apologetic, and I catch a small smile at the corner of his mouth. A glint of pride hides behind his eyes as I force myself into a form of confrontation. The shock of the revelation overtakes the fear and panic that so often swamp me in these situations.

I can't remember ever reading another male romance author.

"Are you alright?" Owen asks. His question plunges me back to this reality. My eyes scan his face and fall over his body, sitting opposite me. I'm caught between desperately wanting to ask questions and running away and making Kez handle any further correspondence. But *I* made myself do this. This was my accomplishment—coming here to meet Olivia. "I didn't mean to mislead you. And I do need an accountant. It's been nice talking to a reader, and I did try and tell you who I was the last time you came in."

"I'm… not comfortable with people. Men." It's the first barrier I put up. The tremble in my hand grows as I reach for my drink and bring it to my lips. Something, anything to distract my mind from the collision course it's currently on.

"As I said, I'm happy to go back to email until you're more comfortable."

His offer makes me pause. Did I want to give this up?

My mind trips over a hundred scenarios, conversations and outcomes that all spiral together into a pressured mess. "Um…"

"So, in the folder I gave you, are all the receipts for Two-

Sided Love. I'm still relatively new at all this, but when the sales picked up and I hit the USA Today list, I knew I had to look into getting my accounts sorted. I've probably missed a load of things.

Work. Keep it professional. That I can do. "I didn't notice anything associated with utilities. If you're working from home, your phone, internet, and other bills can go against your expenditure."

"See, this is why I needed you. I'll send you the HMRC form now as well. It has my actual details on it and I knew I needed to tell you in person."

I nod, struggling to focus my mind on work and not the riot of stray thoughts bombarding me.

Owen—the guy sitting across from me, is the author who wrote the words that sang to my heart. This man has been the only one to draw any response from me, even if it was only my name. Is that a coincidence? I can't think that way.

"What are you thinking?" Owen asks.

"Have you set aside a percentage of all of your income for your tax bill?" The business response is the last thing on my mind, but right now I need to cling to something safe. How can I take anything that this man says as truth after the last few weeks? He's lied about his identity, not only to me but to everyone who's read his story.

"Yes. I knew I'd have to." He sips his coffee looking perfectly comfortable. I wish he didn't. His ease makes me anxious, and I can't help shifting in my seat. George makes a growly yawn and looks up from his bed on the floor. He looks around and casually walks over to introduce himself to Owen.

"Hi there, boy. Aren't you a handsome fella?" He scratches George's head that ensures he falls into his good graces.

"This is George. I'll be able to do all the work for the accounts in the next couple of weeks. I can email you if I have any further questions." My words close the door to further questions or conversation, and I'm torn between needing to retreat and wanting all the new experiences I thought I'd gain by stepping out and meeting Olivia.

I war with myself for a few moments, mentally weighing up the pros and cons of sticking it out here. The minutes tick on, and Owen seems comfortable taking his time, waiting for me to say something. It should be an awkward feeling, but there's no sign he's uncomfortable.

"When did you move to Tregethworth?" The words run together as I fire them out. I use the question as camouflage to check my phone and fire a quick message to Kez. If this isn't enough of a reason for a plea for help, I don't know what is.

"About three months ago. I love this part of the world, and I've slipped easily into the stereotypical lifestyle of a writer hiding away in their home."

"Apart from coffee," I add.

"Apart from coffee. Although I've been known to visit the Kings Port as well."

I nod, wracking my mind for something more business-orientated to discuss.

"Can I get you another cup?" Owen nods at the half-drunk coffee on the table. My phone chimes and I see Kez confirm she's on her way.

"Um, I'm okay."

"Sure?"

I nod, and he smiles back at me, and for the first time, I really notice him. His smile shows a dimple on the right side of his mouth. For a split second, all my worries vanish, and I'm left feeling light and calm for the first time outside of reading a book.

Owen turns away from me, and it's like he's taken all the warmth of the room with him. He goes to place his order, and with his movement, the noise of all my doubts rush back into my head, obliterating the moment of clarity.

My feet itch to stand up and run. To forget about today.

"Hey!"

"Oh, god! Kez, you scared me." Her appearance has me gasping for breath.

"Sorry. So, what's the emergency?" She looks around as if something will pop out and enlighten her.

"I met Olivia. Wait, how did you get here so fast?"

"I was on the way already. What's the problem?"

"Olivia is actually Owen," I mumble the answer, the betrayal still raw in my chest.

"Owen, as in the guy you met? From here?"

I nod and motion towards the counter. "Oh my." She squeezes my hand in a silent offer of strength. "What do you want to do?" she asks.

My answer is a shake of my head, unsure of what I want versus what I've been programmed to do for so long.

"Don't run. You're here. You've obviously had to have some sort of conversation with him. Just focus on that."

I nod, searching for anything close to the courage I need

to walk through this seemingly easy task.

"Hi." Owen returns and places his drink on the table. "I'm Owen. I'm going to take it that you work with Ellie?"

"Yes, my name's Kerenza." They shake, and Owen sits down again.

"A Cornish name. I take it you're local?"

"Yes, actually. Most of my life." Kez's answer is more guarded than I'd expect from her. There's a frost to her tone that is unusual.

Owen sits back in his chair as he did before Kez's arrival and just waits. He doesn't push a topic of conversation. He drinks his coffee and gives me a polite and friendly smile when he catches me looking.

The intrigue and excitement about meeting Olivia is there, under my skin, it's just my head that's kept it in check, and I'm fighting with the concept that I can have those same feelings for a man.

I hold my coffee between my palms and flick my nail on the handle, waiting for someone other than me to break the silence. Kez keeps looking between Owen and me, and I can see the cogs whirring away in her brain. Her auburn hair is free from any other colour this week and catches the lights from the ceiling. When she doesn't realise anyone is watching, she drops her guard and can show the diffident side of her personality. The mature young woman I've grown to love.

"So, Owen, you're the mysterious Olivia Wren." Kez starts. "Kinda shitty you pretended to be someone you're not." She folds her arms across her chest and waits for a response.

"I guess I deserve that."

"Yeah, you do."

"Kez," I caution. I don't want her going overboard and running Owen off, and it's that truth that makes me realise that despite everything, I *do* want to know more. I want to have the experience I thought I'd have with Olivia, even if that means I'll need to have those conversations with Owen. Now that Kez is here, I know nothing will happen or, if I panic, I can leave and not have to worry.

"Have you always been a writer?" My words sound timid and unsure rather than betraying the curiosity that's behind them.

"Umm, no. And honestly, sometimes I still struggle to think of myself as a writer."

"I'd say publishing a bestselling book makes you a writer."

"It could be a lucky fluke. I'm no Stephen King or J.K. Rowling."

"Are you writing more?" This time I muster some strength behind my question.

"Yes. At the moment actually. I've started another story, plus one is in the process of being published. It should be out in the next couple of months."

"Both as Olivia Wren?" Kez chimes in.

"Yes. There's a huge percentage of authors who write under a pseudonym."

"I'm not sure if they all pretend to be members of the opposite sex." Her challenge turns the conversation frosty, and I can feel that place I'd been working to find—where I'm not desperate to run away—is slipping.

"Ellie, do you have everything you need to get started? You have my email, so if you do need anything, please contact me." Owen gives me a pointed stare, looking deep into my eyes. My body burns with the intensity, but I can't pull away. I nod, frightened for a whole other reason. The hazel specks in his eyes sparkle like bronze catching in the sunlight. They cast me in a warmth that's comforting and familiar, without being stifling. It's the opposite reaction to any I've had around a man in years.

Owen stands, smiles, and leaves.

I let out a breath as if I'd been submerged in water for the last two minutes. I draw several deep breaths into my lungs and notice my hands beginning to shake as I put the coffee back on the table.

"That guy. I'm so cross for you, Ellie."

"It's fine," I whisper through pants. Although it's not. Not at all.

"What do you mean, it's fine? You've been looking forward to this for days, and then you find out it's all a hoax. How's that alright?"

Her words are true, but there's a part of me that wants to see the positive side to the situation. "It's not a hoax as he admitted it as soon as we were due to meet. It's just not what I had planned. It pushed me out of my comfort zone, which is what you've wanted me to do for such a long time. And I still want to know all the same things as I did when I knew I was meeting Olivia."

"Oh." Kez wasn't expecting my response, I can tell.

"Thank you for coming to my rescue. I did need the backup, but I think I've made the hardest step. I showed up, and we had a conversation."

"Are you going to see him again?" Kez's face lights up like I've just given her the best present in the world.

"I don't know. I'm torn between what my head and my heart want. But at least now I know I can do it. Or at least attempt it again." I give her a smile and look at George. "Come on, George." I stand, and George shakes himself awake. "I'll see you later, okay."

I walk out of Molly's and onto the beach. I let George run and choose only to see the positives that have come with today. One step forward, one day at a time. That's what I need to work on, and that's what I want to do.

EIGHT

I open the curtains to the day and am filled with a surge of purpose that has previously escaped me.

"Come on, George. Run time." He perks up immediately and jumps up to encourage me.

The autumn sun casts a watery hue of yellow across the sky. I've not been out for the past week, and I can feel my legs growing restless. The amount of time I spend sitting makes running, or at least regularly walking, a necessity.

We walk out and along the path that takes us to the headland before breaking into a jog. It's a steady climb and a safe track to run with George. My pace starts to quicken, and I find my rhythm. As we climb the incline, the view back over Tregethworth is breathtaking. The wind swirls around me and forces me onward to keep warm.

Halfway around the headland, the bright inky sky of the morning conceals the real intent of the weather. Icy splashes of rain begin to coat my face and arms as I pump my legs harder. They chill me through to the bone, despite how hard I'm working. I have at least half an hour left of my route back along and down to the road taking us into

Tregethworth.

George barks his annoyance at the rain, and I agree with him. "I'm sorry, boy. Keep going or turn back?"

His woof and reluctance to continue, tell me he's decided to call it a day. I turn to head back the way we came. At this time of year, it's inevitable to get caught in the rain. The weather does whatever it chooses to, regardless of my plans.

By the time I'm back home, my T-shirt clings to my skin, and my feet make a squelching noise in my trainers. I throw a towel over George and manhandle him in the kitchen before he curls up in the bed and forces me to change the sheets.

After a hot shower that thaws out my freezing limbs, I grab my Kindle from the side and retreat under the covers.

I flick through the first few pages of a new book. As my eyes take the words in, my mind isn't on the characters that I'm getting to know. It's on Owen.

Owen,
I wanted to say sorry about Kez. She is protective of me. It feels a little odd addressing you as Owen now. I enjoyed getting to know Olivia.
Ellie

It's an impulsive email, but I feel better having sent it, although, I now relegate myself to sit and wait for a response. George jumps up and curls at the foot of the bed, settling down now he knows where I'll be for the next few hours.

Ellie,

Again, I'm sorry that I deceived you. Writing under a pen name is a business decision. One that allows a certain amount of protection. I didn't realise we'd strike up a friendship so fast, or that my cover story would cause you alarm. I promise there was never meant to be deceit. I enjoyed our conversations over email. There's a connection I don't want to ignore. We can go back to the emails if you're more comfortable.

Owen

Owen,

You've dropped the O at the end of your emails, I see?

Ellie

Ellie,

I didn't want to deceive you further than I had to. It was a small gesture you were unaware of. I like that you noticed though.

Owen

My cheeks warm reading his words. I hear them in my head in his low, basey voice, and I like it. Reading the words on the screen is safer than in person, and I feel closer to them in some way, like they're the words from the story I'm immersing myself in.

I wanted to talk to you more.

If you have a question, I'll be happy to answer it.

Okay then, Owen, why do you write romance and as a female author?

Technically that's two, but I'll let you have it.
I write romance because I'm an eternal optimist and no matter what, I believe in love. As a guy, it's not a popular opinion to have or share. So, I don't. I can if I'm a woman and a pen name allowed this. Simple as that.

I read his words over and over, committing them to memory. *I'm an eternal optimist, and no matter what, I believe in love.* Is it that simple? Surely not.

The scepticism about a man writing romance is likely to be a popular feeling, no matter how good he might be as a writer. Him having an ulterior motive is the conclusion that people may jump to. And my own favourite: trust. If I wanted to build any kind of friendship with Owen, I'd need a bucket load of trust, and any that had been built has shattered into dust with his revelation. There's a mountain of barriers in our way.

That's a nice notion to write by. I wish life were as simple as believing in something.
Ellie

Sometimes it can be. It's what inspired Two-Sided Love.

You certainly put us through it. There was a point where I didn't think Paul would ever get Shell.

Have faith—an eternal optimist, remember? Sometimes it just takes a little longer to reach the happy ever after.
Will you meet me again? The Waterside for lunch this time?

My heart flutters in my chest at his words. They aren't the same as the words written in the book, but it's like he's talking to my soul. Connecting with a part of me that's been locked away and starved of light and affection for three years.

Can I meet him again? My brain is rattling between options, and my heart is involved in the decision for the first time in years. How was I going to get any better by hiding away?

Intrigue burns through my body, but wanting to go is against everything I've done these last few years.

Okay. Let me know when.

My fingers dash the words out, and they send my heart beat bouncing in my chest at the thought.

We agree on the details to meet later in the week, I turn my phone off and pick up my only other distraction, forgetting about the bravery I need to muster.

The days drag, and the weather casts them in a gloom that is so familiar in Cornwall. I take the day to get into the figures of Owen's paperwork and have a draft set out in the first few hours.

Even for me, I'm starting to get cabin fever, so I walk down the narrow stairs into the shop.

Alec is talking to Kez at her desk. He takes a moment to register my presence, but it's not quick enough for me to see the adoration that shines from his eyes directed firmly at Kerenza.

"Hey, Ellie." He steps back and waits for me to approach.

Alec has been in the shop more regularly than I had first thought when we made the agreement. He's transformed the drab interior, and it now looks like a professional space. Like a gallery space. His work captures the scenery with such clarity—the photographs are filled with emotion and atmosphere as if they're talking to you. His biography states that he's shown his work around the world, but this is his home, and he has a following. Having a permanent space is what he's wanted and means I can keep Kez. She's agreed to handle all of that side of the business, and it keeps her busy when the accounting side is a little quiet. Which is all too often.

Kez beams a welcoming smile at me, and I wonder if she has a soft spot for Alec as well? "Hey, boss. How're things? We've been quiet, but I'm not surprised with the turn of the weather. I'm happy to take George out along the beach though if you'd like?"

"I took him out for a quick walk this morning, but I

know he's not going to say no to you. Come up after you close up shop."

"Okay. Anything else planned for the week?" She busies herself with the few papers on her desk and clicks the mouse. Music starts to play from the small wireless speakers positioned in the corners of the gallery section. It's an odd collaboration—gallery-come-accounting office—but I'm proud of it, or rather Kez, for making it happen.

"I'm going to meet with Owen again."

"Owen?" She whips her head to me and pins me with quizzical eyes.

"Um, yes." I shift my feet, clinging to the confidence I've found over the last few days.

She continues to scrutinise me, and then her whole body changes. Relaxes. "Okay." She goes back to the screen without another word.

"I'm just gonna… go." Alec slips out the front door.

"Hey, is everything okay?" I ask Kez.

"Sure. I'm fine."

"It doesn't sound like you are."

"I just… I don't want you to get hurt. And I'm worried that this guy—because he's written something you love, could take advantage of you."

"Really? Wow. I don't see it like that. Sure, he deceived me. But I understand his reasons. Is it a huge step for me to do this? You bet. But I can't be the victim all the time. You've shown me I need to do more. Little steps forward are the only way, and I need to take them. Even when they're intimidating."

My little pep talk invigorates me, and the confidence

I've been building takes on a new high.

Kez cracks a beautiful wide smile, and I'm left feeling a little confused. "Now I know I don't have to worry about you," she says smugly.

"I'm sorry?"

"Well, your first meeting with him ended in you calling in for reinforcements. Of course, I'd be worried about you going for lunch. But hearing how positive you are, means I don't have to be concerned. You've made the decision, and you're sticking by your conviction. It's all good."

A warm smile graces my lips at her words, and I see how smart she's been. I head back upstairs and resume reading my next happily ever after.

NINE

Tregethworth is a small village with only a handful of shops and stores. After living here for over three years, you'd think I'd have frequented them all and be on a first name basis with each of the proprietors. However, that is not the case. I've visited Molly's often enough. I do the accounts for The Silver Tree and the surf shop. I haven't got past the door of the pub and, before today, I've only visited The Waterside once before.

It's a cute place with a casual café at the front of the shop, and more of a bistro feel towards the back. I arrive a few minutes late, so I don't worry myself silly waiting for Owen. The smell of seafood and garlic is welcoming, and it talks directly to my stomach.

Owen stands at the round table he's chosen, off to one side. It's situated in the café side. Just.

"Hi, is this alright?" He moves around and pulls out my chair for me. His smile displays his dimple, and it lightens his whole face.

"This is fine, thank you." I slide into the seat and take a breath, urging the knots in my stomach to relax. My back's to the door, and I can hear people coming and going. I fight the anxiety within from bubbling up and making me check over my shoulder.

"Here." Owen stands and moves around the table. "Swap. I can see you want to keep an eye on the door. It's fine." I look up into his eyes and see a depth of understanding I never thought possible from a guy.

"Thank you," I mouth the words, unsure if my voice will fail or not. We take our new seats, but now my eyes want to linger on Owen rather than rush to the door. His skin is warm and matches his rich eyes. My lashes flutter as he notices me watching him, so I pick up the menu and flick over the front and reverse.

"What would you like to drink?" A young waitress comes over to our table.

"Ellie?" Owen gestures to me.

"A sparkling water please."

"Make that two." She nods and disappears, and I'm left alone with Owen.

It feels like my first date ever. Awkward, but exciting. I'm thrown back to my teenage years when I dated Billy Young and went to the cinema and out for pizza afterwards.

My confidence has grown, but conquering my anxiety isn't as simple as just knocking it down. It's like a dark shadow, hovering on the peripheral of my life, always ready to invade and block out the sun, just as soon as it's given the chance. It's a constant fight and one I've been happy to lose for the last few years.

Thanks to the words I've read, and the opportunity I have in front of me, I want to push the clouds back for once.

At least for long enough to enjoy this time.

I sit up a little taller and smile at Owen.

"I'm really pleased you felt you could join me today." He keeps his eyes cast on the menu.

"So am I. It's much easier for me to talk through emails."

"I know."

"I've got a draft of the accounts worked out. Two-Sided Love did really well."

"It did. It was a bit of a surprise considering I'm an unknown. At least as Olivia Wren."

"That sounds like you have more stories written." I'd love to read more of Owen's words if they're as gripping as Two-Sided Love.

"A few years ago, I had a couple of books published, but they were written under my actual name, O. Riggs."

"Which explains why I couldn't find anything else for Olivia Wren."

"Correct."

"So, how did you come up with Olivia Wren?"

"It's my Mother's maiden name. Wren that is. And Olivia was close to Owen. No big mystery, but I needed to separate myself from my previous work."

"I didn't see anything relating to income for those other books."

"Honestly, they weren't very successful. And getting the information about sales out of my publisher after the first year was more effort than it was worth. Let's just start with the slate clean."

The waitress drops by with our drinks. "Are you ready to

order?"

"Okay, Ellie?"

"I'll have the crab cakes and salad please."

"And I'll go for the carbonara."

She scribbles on her pad and leaves us again.

The awkward-date vibe returns, but that's preferable to being anxious and nervous in Owen's company. And surprisingly, I'm not. A sense of pride washes relief over me.

"So, when is the next book out, and is that under Olivia again?" *Please say yes, please say yes…*

"Yes, it's under Olivia. You can expect all the same elements as Two-Sided Love." I smile widely, excited to sink into his words again. Each time I think of him as the author, it becomes easier. My body leans in closer of its own accord. It's the closest I've voluntarily been to someone of the opposite sex for quite some time like I'm being pulled in to Owen, rather than fighting to run away as I so often do.

"What about your old author life? Will you write under that again?" Each new fact pushes me to ask another question and to learn more.

"I'm working on that now. O. Riggs takes a darker path than Olivia. Which is another reason for the switch of names. Different markets."

"Darker?" I immediately chill at his words. I want the fantasy world he's created as Olivia—the one that I can hide in, live in, and dream about. I stay away from dark at all costs. I've had enough of that in my real world.

"It doesn't have much romance in the story. It might not be what you're looking for." He looks a little saddened to admit that to me.

I reach for my drink and take a sip.

The door opens, and my eyes flash upward in a moment of weakness. A group of men saunter in, laughing and joking. Their arrival douses me in cold water and my usual reaction and aversion to venturing outside returns. My nerves vibrate and my muscles tense. Men together can be intimidating to any woman. But for me, they remind me of how small and weak I am when trying to protect my body from the hideous acts they want to inflict.

I sink into the seat and make myself as indistinct as possible. I wish I were invisible as they walk past and choose a table at the back.

"Four bottles of bud over here, love," one of them calls out. My eyes fly wide at the thought of the poor girl, who's probably only in her early twenties, having to deal with them on her own.

"Ellie?"

"Pardon me?" I look up and stare right into Owen's eyes. Concern is all I see. It's written all over his face. "I'm sorry?"

"Don't be sorry. You okay?"

"Yes. I'm fine, thank you." I smile through the lie and force my spine to straighten. It's no use though. With every crack of laughter, I hear the voices of the men who attacked me echo in my ears—the jeering and ugly words as I lay beaten and bruised on the ground.

My heartbeat rockets as the memories fuse in my mind's eye.

"Ellie, look at me. At me. Here." Owen grabs my hands from their grip on the edge of the table and forces all my attention on him. "Focus on me. Nothing else."

I nod, but it's not working. The panic creeps up my back, and my hands begin to shake in Owen's.

"What helps?"

"Outside. The sea. It's my escape." I speak my plea softly but wish I could scream it aloud.

"Let's go then." He stands up, pulling me to my feet. He drops a few notes on the table and then lets me lead out of the door. As I burst into the open air, I release the breath I'd been holding.

Owen takes my hand, and I let him. He walks me down the few steps of The Waterside and along the path into the village and onto the beach. When we reach the sand, he lets my hand go, as if it was his job to escort me to safety.

And that's what he did.

TEN

We walk in silence for a while. I wish I had George with me as a distraction, but I wasn't sure he'd be welcome at the café for lunch. He was also my excuse for the meeting to only last a couple of hours. Maximum.

I concentrate on letting my feet sink into the hard-packed sand on the beach and leave my footprints in our wake. The roar of the waves breaking provides a soundtrack to our silence. But I don't feel rushed or the need to fill the quiet between us.

The beach is near empty with only a few others milling about on a dreary day. The wide expanse of sand and sea make it easy for me to see the people around, unlike in a closed in space.

"Are you hungry?" Owen asks. Of course, I'm starving, but I don't want to admit that right now. He leads us towards Molly's at the other side of the beach. "I'm just going to grab a takeaway sandwich or something. You don't need to come in with me." He smiles and disappears inside, but I catch him at the door, looking back towards me.

My mixed-up head is torn between wanting to stay and salvage something of today and just giving up, going home and reverting back to email. But then I won't have gained anything.

"Here." I'm still arguing in my mind about what I should do when Owen hands me a takeaway cup and box.

"What's this?"

"A hot chocolate and a portion of chips. It's not crab cakes, but I thought it might warm you up. And if you don't want them, I'll eat them." He unwraps what looks like a bacon sandwich and takes a bite.

My fingers flip the little cardboard box open, and the sharp smell of vinegar over hot chips assaults my senses. Saliva pools in my mouth, and I pick one up, glad for the food.

"Thank you. This is perfect." I mean it. Owen sits at one of the outside benches, and I follow. Each small gesture, every time he lets me be, he restores part of the trust that he first gained as Olivia. How he looked out for me today is something I'd expect of Kez. Not from someone I've just met.

"So," I start, swallowing a chip and taking a sip of the warm chocolate. "What's the next Olivia Wren book about and when will I get to read it?" It's the most forward I've been since first meeting Owen.

Owen looks at me with a grin displaying his dimple. It also gives him a playfulness that I like.

"Unrequited love. It's a sad story through most of the book actually, but the hero finally moves on and finds his love. As if it was the act of giving up that gave him the space in his heart to find it all over again."

There. In that description, something shifts inside of me towards Owen. Like he's passed some imaginary test to determine that he's not a threat and my mind and body have finally given him a pass.

The thought of reading it has my heart racing, desperate to understand Owen's feelings on the subject. Then I remember that this is a fiction book. Just because he's committed something to paper, doesn't mean it's a true reflection of how he feels. Although it certainly makes me wonder. I can't wait to devour the story.

"That sounds like something I'll enjoy reading."

"Great. There's a certain amount of pressure after the success of my last. I just want to write and enjoy it. Do you want an early copy? It's with the editor as we speak, but I'll get something sent across when it's back."

"You'd do that?" I can feel my eyes widen in wonder.

"Of course. I'd love your opinion. Especially since you read the first book." The smile I give Owen is uncontrollable, and sheer joy, untainted by my past or my memories, blazes over me.

"That's a pretty sight," he says, before looking away from me and towards the surf. I follow his eyes down the beach. The waves crash against the cliff edge like they do every day.

"It's beautiful here. There's a sense of freedom and escape that I've never known before. It gives me room to breathe."

"That's good." He turns back to me, and our eyes meet. The warmth of his eyes is addictive, and I force mine away.

The chips in my hand are suddenly very interesting.

The conversation grows open and easy. That seemed an impossibility a few days ago, and it's somewhat confusing. Giving myself room to enjoy Owen's company means I've actually enjoyed it. The dark part of me assumed I'd never have that, and it's confusing my head.

"As much as I'd like to stay out here all day, I need to get back home. Words need to be written."

"Oh, of course. Don't mind me."

"Let me walk you back. You haven't got George with you."

His simple deduction sends a pulse from my heart to every nerve ending in my body. I nearly sag in relief that I don't have to explain and that this man seems to understand something that's become as much a part of my personality as my physical appearance.

We meander back up to the road and around to the shop. I lead him to the entrance of the gallery, as he already knows that's my base.

"I'm sorry about lunch. Maybe we can stick to coffee or chips on the beach?"

"I'd like that."

There's a pause where I busy my eyes, not sure where I should focus.

"I'll look at getting you the book as soon as possible." He turns and heads back towards the beach. He doesn't look back, and I feel a stab of panic that I might have offended him.

"Thank you," I call out after him. He twists, and I see him smile, offer a wave, and set back off.

I slip around the back and up the steps. I can't face Kez right now. My mind is reeling from today. Confusion and hope cloud my mind. Hope because I've made more progress despite the upset at the café. Those situations are always going to set my mind delving back into my memory. If I'm going to grow, it's the positives I need to learn from.

My eyes shut as I'm hit with a weariness that is so heavy it stuns me.

It's not the feeling of intimidation that has stayed with me, but rather the growing sense of ease and comfort in Owen's presence. That's not me. I've had to work at letting people close to me. And that's only been Kez, really.

My phone vibrates in my pocket, and I'm immediately fumbling for it. When I see my mum's name on the screen, all sense of hope and positivity is crushed inside my chest.

Since the fight three years ago, there has only been a handful of conversations. I've not been back to visit often, and they've not ventured to Cornwall. Of course, they don't understand why I can't come back, and the wedge that has formed between us has only grown wider with time.

"Hi, Mum." I don't mean for my voice to sound so dejected, but I can't keep having the same argument with her.

"Hello, Ellie. How are you?"

"Good, thanks." I don't elaborate and wait for the reason she phoned.

"Okay then. I'll cut the chitchat. Amy is getting married. She and Trevor got engaged in the summer, but now they're setting the plans for the wedding. Amy would like you to be a bridesmaid, but I've suggested that shouldn't be your role in the wedding considering the circumstances. I thought I'd give you a chance to congratulate your sister and talk to her about your reasons yourself."

My little sister is getting married.

"Thank you." Wow. Amy always wanted to get married. She was just as focused on her career as I was, but she fought for love just as much. She'd fit right into one of the stories I read.

"Take care, then." She hangs up. No further conversation, and why would there be? She's made her own decisions regarding my absence.

Married. Wow. She'd only just met Trevor when I visited last year. We'd also grown distant. Sure, there was the odd text message now and then, but it was hard to stay close with such a chasm between us, and I don't just mean physically.

The news has me thinking of the characters in the story I'm reading. The hero is adamant he doesn't want to marry and, of course, the heroine is feeling the crushing disappointment that she can't change the hero's mind. I know it has a happy ending, so I'm looking forward to reading what happens in their story to change the state of play.

When I was in the hospital, I was filled with a hatred that bubbled under the surface, poisoning my view of men. While I've tried hard to dilute that feeling, even being vulnerable with a man sends my nerves scattering around my body, and not in a hearts-and-roses way.

That doesn't mean I can't be happy for Amy, though.

I hear congratulations are in order. Wow! I'm happy for you. Xx

Drinking alcohol usually results in bad dreams, and so I've avoided it for the most part, but I think I might have to indulge in a glass of wine tonight. A toast to small steps and big leaps of faith.

ELEVEN

The smell, earthy and cold mixed with the sharp hit of alcohol wakes me. I pull my arms to hold my weight, but they don't move. My lips part to shout but my face is pushed back down into the ground as fingers start to crawl up my legs. I twist and turn my body to move, to escape, but nothing happens. I can't move and the scurrying of fingers doesn't stop as they grow closer to the apex of my thighs. My lungs burn as my heart thumps in my chest, and I try to suck the oxygen I need in through my nose. It hurts. My body. Everything hurts, and I remember why. Tears of salt and sadness slip past my lashes and into my mouth.

I gasp, and all I get is a mouthful of pillow. All my muscles jolt into action, and I push away from the bed and scamper to the other end. My limbs are all free, and I run my hands over myself checking for rope. Nothing. But the tears are real. My face is damp. I wash them away and force myself to stand to reach the bedside lamp. It casts the room in soft light, banishing the shadows from the corners of the room.

As my reality settles, so does my heartbeat. George looks at me with a sleepy expression on his face. "Sorry, boy. Go back to sleep." My fingers scratch his ears and settle him. Honestly, it helps me as much as he enjoys it.

I slip my feet into my raggedy old slippers and shuffle into the kitchen to make a cup of coffee. With the memory so close to the surface, I won't be able to fall asleep anytime soon. The rich smell fills the kitchen and takes away the scent of alcohol that's stuck in my nose.

My corner chair calls to me, and I take my Kindle along with the mug of coffee and pull the fleecy throw from the back of the sofa and make a nest. Within a few lines, I'm back in the head of the heroine, longing for love and happiness.

Something wet tickles my hand, and I snatch it away. Even half-conscious, I'm in protective mode. My eyes crack open, and George nuzzles my hand.

"Morning, what time is it? I bet you want to go out."

His woof at my words forces my legs to un-tuck themselves so I can stand and let him out. I glance at the clock and see I've slept through half the morning. A quick look and I see that the bed is still in the mess I left it in last night.

Wine. Two glasses and I'm a wreck. I yank the fridge open and proceed to pour the offending liquid down the sink.

After seeing to George and grabbing a shower, I curl back up in my chair and pick up the Kindle from the floor. It must have slipped from my grasp at some point this morning. If I can finish this story, then I can focus on the day job.

Unsatisfied, I flick the last page and sigh. The story had promise, but it just didn't have the heart that I've been wanting or looking for since reading Olivia—or rather Owen.

Owen,
I've just finished a new book. You'll be pleased to know the title of best read of the year still has your name on it. I was wondering if you'd like to meet up again? We can try for food again perhaps? My treat, as a way of an apology considering my track record.
Speak soon, Ellie

As Kez has never been too fussed about books, I've not been able to get excited with anyone about what I'm reading before. With Owen, it's different. We share a common interest, and I find myself wanting to talk to him more and more about it.

Ellie,
I'm pleased to hear that. Knowing you loved Two-Sided Love means a lot. I'm afraid I'm chained to my desk for the rest of the week. Deadlines. Can we rain check and meet after the weekend?
Owen

After last night, the disappointment is sharp. I need to push my feelings back under the surface and focus on something positive. That Owen is the first person I wanted to contact this morning is startling, but it's only because this is so new. I'm not used to having friends.

> Owen,
> Of course. Sorry. Let me know when you're free. I'll look forward to hearing all about the story you're working on.
> Ellie

I shut off the computer and grab my running gear from the dryer and change. Five minutes later, George is jumping up at the door to get going. I take my usual path, up and over the headland. A patchwork of moss green and russets blanket the undulating landscape as I pass. I focus on my surroundings, or on George leading the way, and where I place every foot. The small details keep my mind from escaping to less comfortable topics, and the regular thud of my feet against the earth is my own metronome.

But as my feet eat up the metres, my gaze is drawn to the sea. Small, black dots bob about in the surf, ebbing and flowing with the tide. I snatch glimpses of them as I split my attention between what's in front of me and the ocean.

People are always talking about how energising and exhilarating surfing is. I haven't seen the appeal as yet, but something about moving outside of my comfort zone has set the wheels in motion in my mind. With each day, the thought has wormed its way into my head and is burrowing deeper and deeper, and now it's firmly rooted.

I open the door into the studio and see Kez talking to an older couple who are looking at one of Alec's pieces. I slip past them and sit at her vacant desk. A few minutes later, with an original photograph sale under her belt, Kez is all smiles.

"Hey, that was our first big sale." She's bouncing with excitement as she comes over to me.

"Congratulations. You deserve it."

"You should give Alec the good news. It is your gallery after all." She nudges my shoulder in encouragement.

"No. This is all you. If you hadn't have pushed me, we might be in a very different place. You can dish out the good news."

"Okay. What can I do for you today, anyway?"

"I wanted to pop in and see how you're doing." I don't lead with the main reason.

"Okay… that's not normally like you though. Anything wrong?"

"No. No, nothing's wrong." I can hear the sulk in my voice.

"Okay, try again. Something's up."

My stomach knots at the thought of admitting to Kez what's got me all out of sorts. "It's fine. Or at least can wait until later." I stand and feel like I'm making a big deal out of nothing. After all, it's just a strange feeling in my chest—like I've forgotten something and can't put my finger on what.

"I'm going to come up after I close. I'll get to the bottom of what has you in a twist. I promise!" Kez calls after me as I scurry away. I close the door behind me and let my head hit the wood.

Sure enough, just after five o'clock, there's a knock at

the door followed by Kez's voice.

I've buried my head in actual work since coming to hide back up here. But the time spent focused has provided a perspective on my embarrassment. It feels important to work out what this feeling is on my own, and now I can name it, I can deal with it. Admitting to Kez that my feelings for Owen are confusing me is a big step—it will give them weight and meaning, and I'm not quite ready to face that, but perhaps I was more willing to try at life. Starting with trying something new and out of the blue. Literally.

I open the door and see a big smile on Kez's face as well as a small box of takeaway. "Bribery, I see."

"I'd like to call it gentle persuasion. But hey, we have to eat." She grins.

"Well come on then." I let her in, and we set about our usual routine, albeit, a little early.

As she takes out the plastic containers and boxes, I fetch the plates, and the pressure of the conversation grows in the quiet between us.

"So, we sold a piece today?" I know the answer but can't take the pressure and need to break the tension.

"Yep. Alec was thrilled. It's a big step and hopefully a sign of what's to come."

"Fingers crossed. I have some other work to do to get things moving as well. Everyone loves social media, and that will be a low cost and easy way to get some promotion going."

"Okay, sure."

We fall back into quiet as we unload the food onto our plates.

"Oh, come on, Ellie. I'm dying here." She gives me her best pouty face, and I know I can't stall any longer.

My plan was simple. Put the words in order and just tell her the truth. My eyes rest closed for a fraction longer than usual as I summon the courage to get the words out. "I couldn't see Owen today, and his rain check disappointed me as I hadn't realised how fond of him I'd grown, so quickly, which was confusing and it made me question a lot of things in my life. I wasn't sure what I should be feeling and if I wanted to share how I felt about the whole thing." I gulp air after spitting all the words out.

"Ellie, you got a little fast at the end there."

"Sorry." I busy myself with the food on my plate rather than look at her.

Kez doesn't say anything further for a while, and I wonder if I hurt her feelings about not wanting to talk to her about this earlier.

All this fuss over a guy. I hate myself for even thinking that after everything I've been through, but it's naïve of me to think he hasn't been the catalyst for some of my motivations.

We take our usual seats in front of the telly, and I keep my mouth busy with the food. I hadn't realised how ravenous I was.

"Okay. I've appeased my stomach, so I can talk now." Kez turns to give me her full attention. "You like this guy? But you're confused?"

"I think *like* might be too strong, but I think getting to know him has led me to wonder. I haven't had a feeling of disappointment in a long time."

"This is all great news. Why were you worried?" Her expectant look fills her eyes.

"Because giving it a voice makes it more real for me."

"And that's scary?"

"Yes. I've hidden from my real feelings for a long time and speaking them out loud is very uncomfortable."

"That's a good thing in my mind. You've bottled so much up ever since I met you. You've not been ready to share, but maybe this is the perfect time to slay the demons you've kept hidden?"

"I'm not sure I'm ready for that. But dealing with Alec, meeting Olivia, or rather Owen, they've all forced me to push past the boundaries I imposed to keep myself safe. I find I'm considering things I've not considered before, like hobbies, or doing something for me." I haven't been proud of myself since before the attack.

"So, embrace it. Grab hold of this new confidence and follow it to where it could lead. I'm not saying you've got to run off with this guy and get married. But what's the harm with going for another drink, or a date? Or something other than locking yourself away and reading."

"I don't date, Kez."

"Well, why not? Who says you can't."

"It was…"

"Nope. Shh. I won't hear it. This is the new Ellie Carter, and I won't let you slip back to what's easier."

Easier? I wish that it were just *easier* to get over my fears and move on with my life. I wish my recovery had been easier. That my body didn't still have scars from my surgery, although it's the mental scars that inflict the most pain and suffering.

"I always appreciated that you didn't push for details, but nothing I do is easy. I had to crawl for hours until I found someone who could help me. My dislocated shoulder screamed in pain. My legs were numb. Every part of my body from the waist down was numb. I dug my fingers into the ground and hauled my dead-weight along until I reached the edge of the road. My eye was swollen shut from the extent of the bruising. Each breath took effort to pull the air into my lungs so I could keep going, but I wasn't going to be left for dead." I pause on my morbid recount. "That wasn't easy, Kez. None of this has been easy."

She reaches for my hand and clasps it between hers. "I'm sorry, Ellie. I'm so sorry, and I didn't mean to imply that you're looking for the easy option. I just, jeez… I want you to keep fighting. I know you're a fighter. You've just told me that."

I nod, not able to look her in the eyes and see the pity I know is waiting for me.

It's the most I've ever shared with anyone about the attack. The hospital staff wanted me to make a statement to the police, but I refused. I wouldn't go over all the evil things that they did to me. And if that makes me weak, then so be it. It was my curse to bear. No one else's.

"Ellie?"

"Hmm?" I look up and see Kez hovering by the door.

"I did the washing up. I'm happy to stay if you want the company." I'm sure I have a confused look on my face. How did we go from having a conversation to Kez being ready to leave? "You sort of zoned out after our talk. I didn't want to disturb you."

"Kez, I'm sorry. I didn't even realise."

"Relax. Don't worry. And for the record, I think you're braver and stronger than you give yourself credit for."

"Thank you."

She slips out, and George begins a gentle snore from his bed.

For the rest of the evening, I resist going to my happy place—whatever world I'm currently reading. Instead, I contemplate all the joy that I could be grasping with both hands. All the opportunities, the friendships and experiences that I've let run past me as I cower away and hide.

When will I have grieved enough? When will the ability to trust return? Shouldn't I have to give a little before I can expect anything back?

The sun pushes up the blanket of cloud shrouding the world. It's yellow light reaching out, turning the grey to a soft pink as the rays grow in strength and vibrancy.

It is beauty in the purest form. I stand and watch from the window to get a better view as the sun stretches out and illuminates the bay. This is my slice of heaven. This is my solace from the world I couldn't face, yet it's starting to feel as though I've shut myself away and hidden, instead of building protection and comfort around me.

No more.

I've let a sliver out—a fragment of the story that haunts my every waking moment, and it has given me the space to believe in more for the first time in such a long while.

TWELVE

After staying awake all night and watching the dawn break in a mini-eureka moment, I'm dead for the rest of the day. I curl up with a blanket and George and watch the waves. For hours, I track the time by the slide of the tide until my eyes are too heavy to pull in any further information.

I want tomorrow to come and to have a good night's sleep because tomorrow will be the start of me working harder for life.

I read until my Kindle runs out of battery, but I don't plug the charger back in. The words can't hold me in the same way as they could a few days ago. The temptation is there, whispering in my ear to just forget everything and escape. Pretend I'm someone else in a world filled with happy and forever. But I owe it to myself to focus on me right now.

The morning arrives far too late for my liking, but I force my legs to move. My mind is telling me to seize this day because if I let it pass; there might not be another chance.

My income is modest, and I'm fortunate that I had

savings when I arrived in Cornwall. They have dwindled, and I should have been keeping a closer eye on my finances. A stupid mistake for an accountant. Gone are the days of fourteen-hour days in London, but somewhere inside of me there's a drive and determination to achieve, it just needs unlocking.

I spend the next few hours going over all the work I need to complete for clients, and I make sure I prioritise it rather than procrastinating in books. One of my first clients when I moved here, The Silver Tree, is all finalised for this year. I think I can count on one hand the times I've spoken to Silvia. The thought is in my head before I can fear it. I'm out the door and walking along the road until I see the small workshop and the gilded sign hanging over the door.

Gentle music plays as I enter. The wooden floor creaks under my feet as I look around the shop.

"Hi, Ellie. Nice to see you." Silvia pops her head out. "Is everything okay?"

"Fine, fine. Thank you. I was just browsing."

"Oh, well, be my guest. Anything in particular?"

Her question has me stammering in my mind. And then it comes to me.

"Um, actually. My sister is getting married, and I'd like to get her an engagement gift. I thought something pretty, maybe a necklace."

Silvia lifts the wooden countertop off the desk and comes into the shop. She bends down to one of the lower shelves and pulls a necklace from it. It's a knot of metal, tied in an intricate and delicate way, sitting at the end of the chain. I love it immediately but can't help and want it for myself.

A shadow catches my eye, and I freeze. A couple walks past the shop front, their muffled voices barely audible, and I let the tension drain from my body.

"You alright, dear?" Silvia asks.

"Yes. I'm fine. Thank you. I love the necklace, but I'm afraid I want to keep it for myself. Do you have something a little daintier?" Amy likes pretty things, and although I found the necklace particularly striking, I'm not sure Amy would agree with my tastes.

Silvia rummages before looking out into the shop. She goes to a small glass display near the till and points out a swath of fine silver threads with pearls attached. Or at least they look like pearls and much more Amy's style.

"Perfect. Thank you, Silvia. May I take them both?"

"Of course, dear. Let me wrap them up."

She ducks back under the table and lays both necklaces on a leather mat and goes about fetching boxes and tissue paper. Silver imprints of a delicate tree are printed on the background.

"It's… the books look really good, Silvia. It's been lovely to watch the business grow," I blurt the words, afraid I'll let the chance slip away.

"Yes, it's been a good season. Of course, the summer is always better. And these new-fangled websites where you can get things directly have helped. I sell online just as much as in person now."

"That's great. Well, I know I'm going to love wearing my new necklace."

There's a pause while she finishes sealing the two boxes

up. My mind races for something to say, but I realise that I can't just turn up and find an immediate friend. Friendships need to be nurtured, as I've done with Kez, so I make an effort and rise above the fear that hampers me.

"I was thinking of getting a takeaway coffee from Molly's. Would you like me to fetch you something?"

"That's a kind offer. I never say no to a hot chocolate. If you don't mind?"

"Of course not." My heart lifts. I hand over my card and take the lovely gift bag from Silvia.

I walk down to Molly's and order two hot chocolates. Before heading back, I stop to look at the waves. I can feel the power of them here—the power of each wave as it crashes against the sand. My lungs fill with the salty air, and I pull my strength down into my guts.

Day by day, step by step, I can push myself back out into the world and really make this my home. Before the hot chocolate turns into a milkshake, I leave the beach and stop back in on Silvia. Her warm greeting tells me all I need to know. I've made the first step and reached out. That's the important part.

My fingers can't stop touching the knot of metal at my throat. It's tactile and comforting. A symbol that I'm going to move forward. It's silly because I feel like a school girl getting excited over something so small as new jewellery, but it's more than that. It's my symbol of strength and courage—both of which I'll need in spades to conquer all my fears and anxieties.

I've been good for the last two days and haven't checked

my email. If I needed to do anything, Kez would have said. I didn't want to look and find an empty screen, or rather, no further contact from Owen. He did say after the weekend though, so I should just try and relax. My breakthrough over the last day has been a good distraction, but I wanted to look and find something from him. I knew I was being optimistic. Two days was nothing when he had a deadline, but the longing for contact wouldn't disappear.

I fire up the computer, but not to check my email. The Google search box fills my screen, and my fingers type the name of the surf school that's located on the beach. They're open all year round, but as it's the off-season, I'm hoping they will have space. With everything that's happened over the last few weeks, I'm waiting for my courage to desert me. Carpe diem, as they say.

A short conversation later, I have a surf lesson booked for myself and Kez with the only female instructor they have. Kez might kill me later, but I know I'll need her support.

Downstairs in the gallery, Kez has her head down and is focused on something on the small screen on her desk. The shop is empty, and so I slip to the door and twist the sign to closed.

"Hey, what are you doing?" She looks up and hits me with a perplexed stare.

"I need to close up for the day."

"Why?" Worry slides over her face.

"Nothing to worry about. I just need you to come with me for a couple of hours."

"Okay, are you going to be any less cryptic?"

"I took your advice. Or rather, I haven't managed to shake the feeling that I'm not living my life, and I suddenly feel the need to take back some control. So I've booked us a surf lesson."

"Surfing? I thought you said…"

"I know, I know, but let's just do this before I change my mind."

"You know I can surf, right? All you needed to do was ask, and I'd have taken you out?" Kez puts all her sass into her 'I told you so' statement, and I feel a little deflated about my master plan, but it doesn't change the intent or that she'll do this with me. Together.

After an hour of wrestling into a wetsuit, getting the feel of the board on the sand and putting some energy into jumping from a lying flat on my tummy position to springing to my feet, we finally get into the water. Kez is right by my side, leading the way, while Jenny, the very patient instructor is waiting on the beach.

The water bites like ice on my skin even through the wetsuit and the first wave that breaks over my head shocks me so much that the air is stolen from my lungs as I attempt to breathe through it.

And all the time, the mantra ringing out inside my mind is that I can survive this. I can do this. I want to do this.

"You know, you weren't that bad." Kez's attempt at encouragement falls far short of what would be needed to get me to try this again. Wave after wave crashing over me and knocking me off balance and into the bitter water wasn't, I decided, the best way for me to seize my life back. The chill that permeated through me to my bones didn't set me free but instead reminded me of my vulnerability.

"I'm not sure surfing is the best means for me to take back some control of my life."

"Well, perhaps something else. Like sea kayaking. It's much calmer, and you're inside a raft. You can paddle along and not worry about the waves so much. Or paddle boarding? Now we have you open to trying out ideas, we should."

The answer I should be striving for is yes. But I feel like I've been dumped out on the beach after being in a washing cycle for the last two hours. The grit and determination that I know are inside of me needs to thaw out and help me see the positives.

"We'll see," I croak out. My throat is raw and parched from the salty water that I swallowed time and time again. "We'll see."

After a scalding hot bath to warm my bones, I consider the accomplishment I made today. Another step forward. It's not about the fact that I hated surfing, it's the effort to *do* something positive that forces me to consider a wider world than the walls around me. Nothing terrible happened, and I didn't have a panic attack. All a plus.

When I've towelled off, my attention returns to the computer and the lack of messages from Owen.

I pace past the machine as if it might bite if I sit down and turn it on too fast. George grows anxious with all the pacing and starts to follow me back and forth.

My phone buzzes on the desk and scares me half to death.

Hey, how you feeling? Warmed up? Do you want me to take George out? Kez

I'm warm, yes. That would be great. I'll put the kettle on when you come up. Maybe we can go together. I just need to dry my hair.

:-)

After a shorter than usual walk on the beach and over the headland, there's nothing more I want to do than collapse and fall asleep on the sofa. A perfect end to any day in my opinion. Being out with Kez and George took my mind off Owen, and I'm surprised she didn't ask about him. She mainly talked about surfing and when she had lessons as a kid. Of course, growing up on the beach, it wasn't a stretch to think she'd be surfing from a young age. There was something nostalgic about her words. As if she were trying to forget part of her memories, or leaving a part of them out.

When we return, my head is clear, and a sense of triumph engulfs me. I peek at my emails to see if he's made contact.

Ellie,

I need a break. I've done nothing but write for the last few days. What about lunch tomorrow? Or a coffee? You tell me. And have you read anything the last few days of note? I rather enjoy holding the best-read category from you, and any insider information on the competition will be gratefully received.

Owen

Owen,

Tomorrow sounds perfect. I'm happy to try for food. You'll be pleased to know I've not read anything that competes with Two-Sided Love. I've had my head inside other books—the accounting kind—the last few days. But, if anything catches my eye, I'll be sure to let you know.

Ellie

Ellie,

Great. I'll pick you up at 12.30 p.m., and we can pop down to the Kings Port. Are you okay with that? I'm happy to take you to wherever you're the most comfortable.

Owen

I can't help the quickening of my heart at his words, although it does feel like he's treading on eggshells around me. That's not what I want, and it's not how I want him to see me—as someone frail. Of course, I've given him nothing but evidence to support that evaluation.

Owen

Thank you. I have to say, you've really helped these last few days. See you at 12.30 p.m.

Ellie

I smile at the screen, but before I can move to go and make a cup of tea, I hear another ping.

Ellie,
This is still in draft form, but I hope you enjoy.
Owen

I click on the attachment and see it's the manuscript of his next book. My finger double-clicks the document, and I curse the time it takes my computer to bring up the book.

I want to curl up in my chair with my Kindle rather than read on the computer, so I do a quick Internet search and manage to send it to my Kindle.

Unrequited by Olivia Wren.

Time slips past me, and so does the need to do anything other than get lost in the pages as I race through the words, desperate to complete the story. Even in draft format, it's engrossing. Every time I reach a new chapter, my eyes have already begun reading the words before my mind can tell me to stop.

Owen is right. It's a sad, melancholy story but one that grips your heart with both hands and has you longing for a happy ending. There are passages of prose that I can feel the optimism Owen spoke of, and it's endearing. I feel a new connection to the story and suspect it's because I know Owen—have talked with him. It's more personal. Like the words are more vivid. And I can totally see him as the main lead, Paul.

The clock on the coffee table glares at me as I force my eyelids open. I must have fallen asleep at some point in the early hours, as it's gone four a.m. already. My legs unfurl from under me, and I stagger into the bedroom and fall into bed.

George's cool nose on my cheek wakes me, and I come around, realising I've slept in. "Sorry, boy. You should have woken me earlier." I pull back the covers and note I'm still in the clothes from yesterday. George cocks his head at me as if to say he doesn't approve. "I know, I know. I'll take care of it."

I let him outside and set about waking myself up with a hit of caffeine. Then I do something about my appearance. I can't even remember finishing the book before falling asleep. The compulsion to go and pick up my Kindle is so strong, but it's already gone 10.30 a.m. If I give in now, I'll still be in yesterday's clothes when Owen arrives. Shower, food, take George out and then maybe I can go back to reading.

At twenty past twelve, my phone buzzes, and I see a text from Owen.

I'm downstairs. Ready when you are.

Faced with seeing him again, I'm thrown into a sudden spin as my nerves rattle my body. My fingers twist the knot of silver at my neck as I try and calm my breathing and control the mini-panic attack.

In my gut, I know it's not just the fact of going out in public and to a place I'm unfamiliar with. It's the growing connection to Owen that fazes me just as much. I pull open the door and battle on, unprepared to let this chance slip away.

Owen is browsing as I come through the door. He's dressed in dark jeans and boots and has a dark jacket on. His hair looks a little wild, and I can't tell if that's natural, or a result of the weather. With his eyes focused on one of Alec's photographs, I can take a moment to watch him.

"Hey, Ellie," Kez calls from her seat, interrupting my perusal.

"Ready to go?" Owen turns and gives me a friendly smile.

"Sure." I hustle out onto the street and attempt to hide my jitters. Owen follows, and as I wait for him to take the few steps to catch up, I feel something within my chest relax. Like all the tension's been released.

He offers me his elbow. I stare at it in bewilderment before I snap myself from my trance and gingerly thread my arm through his. Such a small, and perhaps old-fashioned gesture, but one that makes me happy inside.

"How are you feeling today? Tired at all?" Owen asks as we head down to the shore.

"Maybe a little, why? Oh, you're fishing?"

"Curious. Of course, if you've not had time to read it..."

"No... I did start last night. I'm just at the bit where Paul is helping Kelly clear out her mother's things. I think. That's the last thing I remember from last night. If I'd picked it up this morning, we'd never get to the Kings Port."

"Do you do that often?"

"What?"

"Stay up reading until you fall asleep?"

"Um, probably more than I should." A shy smile creeps across my lips as I admit it.

"You need to remember to take care of yourself as well as your reading habit."

"You're a writer. You're supposed to love readers like me. We're your biggest fans," I protest.

"Point taken." He doesn't push for my opinion or thoughts on the book. Inside, I'm desperate to gush about how brooding Paul is, and how I hope Kelly figures out that he's her soul mate. But I also want to be calm and objective about the book. Owen trusted me with an early draft, and I want to do it justice.

We're quiet for the rest of the short walk around the headland to the Kings Port. It's quiet, given it's a Monday lunchtime. We're seated in the restaurant end of the pub, away from the crab pots and nets hanging from the ceiling in the main bar area. It's a traditional Cornish pub, full of charm and charisma, but I'm immediately looking around and checking how far the exit is from our table.

The window across the room shows off a perfect vista of the ocean with part of Tregethworth framed to the side. The steps leading up to the pub give us the height needed to look down on the beach below.

"Your hair suits you like this," Owen comments, snapping my attention back to him.

"Oh, thanks." I take one of the ringlets in my hand

and try to force it behind my ear with little success. It just bounces back around my face.

"What would you like to drink? A glass of wine, perhaps?"

"No, just a cranberry juice for me please."

"Coming up. I'm going to order at the bar and grab us a couple of menus."

I nod and reach for my necklace. It's so weird. It's like I've worn it for my whole life. It's almost instinctual to hold it as a way of anchoring me.

"New necklace? It's striking." Owen is back before I realise he's been gone.

"Yes. It's a piece from one of my other clients. The Silver Tree."

"Can't say I've stopped in, but it certainly suits you." The warmth of my cheeks filters through my body at his compliment. He hands me the small menu, and I scan the offers. It's an easy choice for me.

"I love Moules marinière with cream and garlic." I can almost smell the garlic and wine already.

"Great choice. I'm going to go for good traditional steak and ale pie."

A young girl, no older than sixteen or seventeen walks up to our table. In a tiny voice, she asks us for our order.

Owen looks at me and raises his brows, a silent check I'm okay. I nod, and Owen delivers our order to the girl.

"All good?"

"Umm hm," I confirm although really, I'm still working on settling myself. A few minutes after she's left us, I start to relax, my shoulders coming down from around my ears.

"That's better." Owen puts his beer down and smiles.

"Sorry, what?" I didn't say anything.

"You've started to relax. It's good. I want you to take your time." For a guy, he's very observant. He seems to be able to pick up on all of my tells and read them just as easily as I read his words.

"Sorry. It takes a while. I'm not great with people."

"Please, don't be sorry. I said we'd take this at your pace, and I'm happy you're still willing to get to know me." He smiles, and it reaches his eyes making them look warm and inviting.

"Sooo," I start, wanting to change the subject. Otherwise, I'll be making a fool out of myself for more than one reason. "Your next book."

"This is where you tell me it's a masterpiece, yes?" he jokes.

"Well, I was going to ask you if you've had experience of unrequited love. It seems so real when you read the emotions on the page."

"I'll take that as a compliment. And some of it is pulled from personal experience. I think most writers use their experiences in one way or another." Owen's eyes cloud over as if he remembers a particularly sad memory. The words to ask more are stuck in my throat, but I can't intrude beyond what he's comfortable to share. If the situation were reversed I know I wouldn't be ready to open up. I doubt I ever will.

"Well, the book is a fantastic follow-up. Just as gripping. If it weren't for sleep or meeting you, I'd have finished it in one sitting." I pause, unsure of how much more to offer.

"That's certainly good to know, and my editor will be

glad."

"Do you enjoy writing all the aspects of romance?" I can't believe I've asked him. The words just popped out of my head.

He gives me a cute smile, and a slight blush rises over his cheeks. He sits back in the chair and rubs the stubble on his chin, hiding his eyes from me.

"Are you referring to anything in particular, Ellie?"

My head is stuck on the steamy scene between Paul and Shell in Two-Sided Love and the brooding anticipation that Paul is currently agonising over. "The points of view? Is it easier to write from the man's because, well, you're a guy?" My questions are the bravest I've been in years.

"It can be hard to be authentic when I'm writing the woman's perspective, yes. Perhaps you can help me when I get stuck in the future?"

"Sure," I squeak. My heart pounds in my chest imagining the conversations we could have. "When is it out? Unrequited, I mean." The questions were getting too personal too easily.

"Oh, a few more months yet. Finishing the book is only half the job. It needs to go through a bunch of stuff. But I don't really get involved too much with that. I'm already working on another story." He takes another mouthful of beer. "So, aside from staying up late reading, what do you like or enjoy?"

It's the most direct question I've had to field in a long while. "Well, reading takes up a lot of my spare time. But I do like to be outdoors. On the beach or the headland. Places I know. With George, of course."

"Now, that's where I get confused as I thought that being outside on your own would accelerate your anxiety? Tell me to mind my own business if you don't want to share." He must have seen the panic in my eyes.

"No, it's fine." I take my time, knowing that Owen would rather wait for the answer than not receive one. "Being outside, at the beach, reminds me that I'm far from the world that hurt me. That I'm on my own and that I don't need anyone. Aside from George."

"Obviously, that's a given," Owen chips in, lightening the sombre direction I'm taking the conversation.

"It gives me the headspace I need to process. Plus it's the most beautiful place in the world." I smile and reach for my necklace, mentally marking off another accomplishment. Being open and honest about something personal is rare, but the longer I spend around Owen, the more of that original trust has started to return.

"I'm sorry I deceived you. If I could take it back and start again, I would."

"Why did you just say that?" I'm sure I didn't speak my thought.

"Because it's the truth."

"No, I mean why then? At that point in our conversation?"

"You looked sad like you'd missed something and wanted it back. Trust is important to you. Much more so than to other people. I threw that away before I even realised I had it, and I can't tell you how sorry I am for that."

My stomach fizzes at his words, and I feel the air in my lungs catch.

The slightest touch against my finger splits my mind. Half wanting to pull away, and the other wanting the contact—real contact—between me and someone else. The only *real* contact in years. I fight to keep my hand where it is on the small table, an inch from his hand, but not out of reach.

"Here you are." The waitress saves my struggle, and I pull my hand back as she places a large pot down in front of me. The heat from the slight connection still radiates on my skin.

A quiet smile softens Owen's face as if he's pleased about something. I keep my thoughts to myself about what that could be.

THIRTEEN

The food, although simple, is delicious. But it's Owen's company that has me enthralled. Just as the pages of his stories have me immersed in his world of emotion and love, I find myself realising that the initial spark I felt with Olivia, was perhaps Owen all along.

Our conversation smooths out over food, and we stray on to other safe topics. It's the most alive I've felt in three years. So much so that I almost forget about the shadow of fear that lurks in the recess of my mind, waiting to grow so large it rules me.

Owen holds the door as I zip up my coat and leave the pub. My heart picks up a beat, not because I'm feeling wary of being out in the open, but because I want Owen to offer me his arm again. I want to feel that pure emotion that lifts my spirit at the connection between us.

But it doesn't come.

"Do you fancy a walk back along the beach? I haven't spent nearly as much time appreciating where I now live as I should."

"I'd love that."

We head off down the coast road that will lead us down onto the sand. The tide is coming in, but we're not at risk of getting cut off as we're not walking the full length of sand. I step over the collection of boulders, the edges softened and worn away from years of erosion. As I jump from the last one onto the sand, Owen holds out his hand for balance, and I instinctively take it. He wraps his fingers around mine and looks me dead in the eyes, waiting for my response. Heat floods me, and I don't pull away. I see the question he's asking me in his eyes—he's asking for my permission, and I give it to him. Freely.

There are no words spoken, just a sense of expectation or maybe excitement that buzzes through me. It's so alien to me, and I find myself wanting to cling onto Owen even harder because of it.

Our steps fall in beside one another, balancing each other's gait and pace. It feels… natural, to walk next to Owen. To feel the warmth of his hand radiate through me. I look out to the surf and take in the air as if it's the first time I've opened my eyes to see what's right in front of me.

We don't talk much on the way back, but his hand stays wrapped around mine with no sign of breaking. The pounding in my chest intensifies as we come off the beach and up the road to the studio. Men haven't been anything other than people to be cautious of for a long time, and now, I don't know how I should act.

Owen steers the way and keeps our hands locked as his eyes take in mine.

His free hand comes up to brush a curl from my face, hooking it behind my ear. Goose bumps erupt across my skin at his touch, and I force my breathing to remain constant. A futile task.

"You're extremely beautiful, Ellie."

His words make it impossible for me to keep looking at him, and I turn away, hiding the scarlet flush that's covering my face.

After a minute, I've regained some composure to look at him again. A charming grin is on his face. His brown eyes are as tempting as chocolate—a day or so of stubble covers his angled chin. Even his Adam's apple is handsome. "I'd like to take you out again."

"I'd like that, too." My heart doesn't ever want to let him go.

"Good. Coffee tomorrow and then dinner Friday? We don't have to leave Tregethworth. We can try the hotel on the road out. I've never eaten there."

"Okay. Sure. I've not been there either. It's a date."

My cheeks ache from the smile I give him in return, and my free fingers clasp the necklace at my throat. Owen pulls my hand away and brings it to his lips. This man is all about gestures, and it's just what I need. He's being gentle and easing me into the idea of anything beyond friendship, and for the first time, that thought doesn't break me out in a frightened sweat. I suddenly have the overpowering need to throw my arms around him and feel how comforting it would be in his. To be wrapped in strength and protection. My soul craves it.

He steps back, dropping my hands and leaving me feeling like a million pounds on my doorstep.

My eyes follow him as he walks around the corner,

and I chicken out of sharing with Kez and head around the back and up the steps from the garden. George greets me, sniffing all over as if checking where I've been. "I know. It's Owen. You like Owen. He's a good guy. You don't need to protect me from him." I pet him until he settles, the words resonating in my mind at how true they really are. George catches on as well and backs off.

I slip down into the chair and let out a sigh filled with the emotional release that's been building.

A lunch date. Nothing serious, yet after only a few hours, I feel so different. A possibility of something exciting is on the horizon, and I want it. It's terrifying but in a making-my-stomach-quiver-with-excitement, way. Anticipation overrules anxiety, and despite the shaky start, I *want* to trust Owen. Like letting a part of me be vulnerable to him is the key to moving forward in general.

I think about Amy getting married. And then I remember my mum and her dismissal of me from the wedding. It's probably for the best. Being with all those people, having to hold it together for Amy would send me racing for safety faster than many of the everyday scenarios that threaten my mind.

The necklace I bought Amy is still on the counter. I need to post it, so I wrap it up and address the padded envelope before taking George down to the little post-office section in Molly's.

Perhaps later, once I've come down from today, I'll talk to Kez.

Knowing I'm here to meet Owen for coffee feels like I have a magical cloak, swathing me with confidence and strength. I still stutter as a couple pass me as I go inside, but once settled, I feel like I'm handling the situation more calmly.

I'm sure I spook Molly when I order my latte. I smile and attempt a brief conversation about the cake choices in front of me. Avoiding physical interactions might have saved me pain, but it also caused severe damage as well. It's not until now that I've noticed how deep the damage runs.

I find an empty sofa facing the glass doors and settle George. I'm at least one coffee cup too early, but I don't care. I want to watch Owen arrive.

The shop is quiet, and my view of the doors out to the deck is uninterrupted. As much as my heart is telling my body it's pleased to be seeing Owen, I still feel a chill slide over my skin when a tall man walks into the shop. He doesn't even look in my direction, but every muscle in my body tightens like a piano wire. My flight reflex is in overdrive even when there is no logical reason for it.

Just before I drain the dregs of my latte, I see Owen head up the deck outside. Before he comes in, he turns to look in the direction I'd arrive from. He pulls out his phone and busies himself for a moment before coming inside. I hear the ping in my pocket and grin.

Kez was right when she first saw him.

Handsome.

Not too smart, with a relaxed way about him. I couldn't see past the fact that he was taller and stronger than me at first. Now my confidence has grown to be able to admire him.

He looks around the shop, and his eyes fall on me in a matter of seconds. "Did I get the time wrong? I thought we said ten thirty?"

"We did. I just wanted to get here early." That fizzing sensation in my stomach starts up again, sending nerves ricocheting through my body for a whole different reason than I've been used to.

"Alright then. What can I get you?"

George puts his head up to see who's come to visit. All he does is go and make a fuss of Owen, who in turn pets and strokes him, firmly setting their friendship in place.

"Just a small latte please."

"Anything to eat?"

"Feel free to get a slice of cake."

"Hey, a man's got to eat. And Molly does a mean carrot cake. So good, I might have to get territorial if you want to share."

"Oh, be my guest. In fact, I will have a slice after all, and we can both be satisfied." The heat in Owen's eyes from my comment sends my stomach into chaos. It's only for a moment, but there's a fierce attraction that I've been blind to until now. He masks his features before heading to the counter. My mouth's gone dry, and my pulse beats heavily in my veins.

Without realising, the connection that had sparked between us is edging towards more intimate waters. A natural progression for some, but one that fills me with a new kind of fear.

I haven't been with anyone since that night. How could

I? It took months of recovery, and the last few weeks have been the first time I've wanted to fight against my body's natural aversion to the rest of the world, including the opposite sex.

Here I am, considering… well, I wasn't considering anything just yet. But Owen has woken my body up with hope.

A part of me died during the attack. When they brutalised me, they killed my sexuality and my ability to make myself vulnerable. I didn't miss sex. I hadn't thought of it past the scenes in the books I read. It was another extension of my fantasy world where the characters got to do all the magical things I didn't. And somewhere along the road I'd grown used to that concept and accepted that. It was safer.

"Two large slices of carrot cake. Plus a latte."

"Thank you." I shake my head and snap myself from my woes. I'd travelled a hundred miles in my head down a road with Owen when I should be focussing on the now.

"You alright? You look a little startled."

I put on my best poker face and eye up the slice of cake, dripping in frosting. "I'm all good. Nothing a healthy dose of sugar won't fix." My voice is flat and cold.

Owen comes around the table and sits down next to me. The sofa is small, and it forces us together. I take a deep breath hoping my body will stay relaxed and calm. The scent of the ocean, crisp and clean, hits my senses and I'm a moment away from humming aloud in pleasure. It's a smell I can take comfort in, and my body relaxes as if it's realised the same thing. He's just what I need to forget my thoughts.

A buzzing from my bag pulls my attention away, but I don't want to be rude.

"Don't worry. Answer it." He nods before leaning back in his seat.

Amy's name flashes on the screen. "It's my sister."

"Really. I don't mind. I have cake."

"No. I can call her back later. I'm not really up for a conversation with her here."

"Oh?" Owen leans forward again.

"Amy, my sister, recently got engaged."

"And I'm not seeing a lot of excitement from you at this." He cocks his head to the side and gets a clearer line of sight to my eyes.

"No, I guess not. I sent her a gift yesterday." I pause and dig my fork through the soft frosting and cake.

"Families can be complicated."

I swallow the sweet mouthful and nod my agreement.

"Hey, I don't want you to be sad. Let's talk about something that will put a smile on your face again."

"Oh, I'm sorry. Amy and my mother can be… difficult. They will probably tell you the same about me. Of course, they don't have a lot to do with me since I moved to Cornwall. They didn't take too well to my moving away."

"I can't quite believe anyone would see you as difficult." He goes to move a curl back behind my ear again, and his touch sparks all the queasy feelings from a few moments ago, just ten-fold. He smiles while holding my eye contact and the bottom of my stomach drops away.

I fight with my body, not wanting to look away, wanting to see if the heat that lingers grows hotter. The second's tick past and neither of us break the contact. Both of us held in each other's gaze. As the time passes, it becomes easier. More natural.

I finally pull my eyes back to my coffee, embarrassed that I was staring for so long. My eyes dart across to Owen, and he wears a contented look. He's always so calm and controlled. Something else that draws me to him.

I need that in my life.

It feels all too soon when the cake is nothing but crumbs on the plates, and the coffee is long gone.

"Let me walk you back?" Owen asks.

"Sure. I'm going to head along the beach first to give George a run."

"I have time." He holds out his hand, and I take it.

Just as the other day, he offers his arm when we're out of the shop, and I loop mine in his. Being this close, I make sure I breathe him in. Each meeting with Owen I grow more familiar with physical contact. It's slowly filling a hole in my heart that I hadn't felt necessary to mend.

We walk along the beach taking a slow, leisurely pace and let George run off before he retreats and checks, and then dashes back out towards the surf again.

Questions and topics of conversation swirl in my mind but I don't have the confidence to ask any of them—the bigger ones: do you have a girlfriend or wife and do you see me as anything other than a friend and a fan? I promise myself that I'll work up to asking him those. Just not today. I have secrets that I'm not about to share with him. I won't be a hypocrite and expect him to answer my intrigues if I'm not prepared to return him the same courtesy.

George paddles his feet and seems happy to leave my side for longer periods. His head still popping back up and looking for me.

"He's protective of you," Owen states.

"Yes. I like him that way. He's my safety blanket in a way. I'd never be able to go out for a run if I didn't have George with me."

Owen nods. I wait for the inevitable questions from my statement, but they don't come.

"As much as I love this, I need to think about getting back. Coffee seems to have turned into lunch as well."

"Yes, sure. No problem. George!" George comes bounding along the beach right up to me. I bend to greet him and tickle behind his ears.

Owen takes my hand and wraps his fingers around mine. I look at him and smile.

"So, are you still okay for dinner on Friday?"

"Um, sure."

"It's a date."

George leads the way back to the studio, and for the first time, I wonder if I should invite him up. I quash the idea before I've finished thinking it through. That's too much too soon.

We pause on the step to the studio and the fizzy sensation in my stomach attacks again. My eyes track Owen's and how they struggle to keep locking onto my eyes, instead, dipping down to my lips.

"I better…"

He leans in and plants a soft kiss on my cheek. It's fast, and he's looking at me with a satisfied grin on his face before

I register he's done it.

"You better?" he prompts. I can hear his smug tone but don't mind. Another day I would have pulled away. Now all I feel like is a giddy teenager.

"I better let you go."

"Only until Friday. I'll pick you up. I'm happy to walk to the hotel, or we can drive."

"Let's see if it's dry. I'd hate to walk in the rain."

"See you Friday, then."

FOURTEEN

"Hey, was that Owen leaving?"

"Yep." My smile is stretched across my face so wide that my cheeks puff out.

"And from that grin on your face, it must have been a good meeting?"

"Yep."

"Oh, come on. You can't leave it at that!" She pouts, and it's adorable.

"I'll put the kettle on and come down for a cup of tea." I hurry upstairs, pet George and make two mugs before coming back down with them. The shop is empty with only the soft music for company. We both move over to the tiny two-seater sofa that Kez has picked up from a second-hand shop. It makes the studio more inviting, and it's certainly a plus for catching up without leaving the shop unattended. We curl up with our drinks.

"So…" Kez prompts.

"So, he's a great guy who seems kind and caring."

"And handsome. Don't forget handsome."

"Yes, he's… handsome." My cheeks flush at my

acknowledgement.

"Yes! You've finally admitted it. This is fantastic. I'm so excited for you." She leans in and squeezes me, clearly enjoying my breakthrough along with me.

"I really like him, Kez," I mutter through a faceful of my locks.

"And I'm pretty sure he's yours for the taking, hun. Don't you be worrying about that."

My previous elated mood takes a sudden crash at the realisation that he may not feel the same way about me. My face freezes and drains of any colour that had flushed my cheeks a moment ago.

"Oh, don't look like that. He's smitten. I'd put money on it."

"Umm-hmm." My heart thumps loudly in my chest, my nerves now spiralling for an entirely different reason than what I've felt for the last three years. All of the emotions bombarding me make it hard for me to think clearly. My gut reaction is to hide away and pretend all of this is just part of another story I'm reading. Yet I'm making steps forward. Fear has held me in a grasp so tight, and I've not known how to break free and simply *be.*

This nervous butterfly feeling is normal. It's probably one of the first normal parts of my life I've had in the last few years.

"What should I do?" I ask Kez softly.

"About Owen? Simple. Keep doing what you're doing. Don't worry about it and let things develop naturally. Don't fight this, Ellie. And don't fear it."

"Easier said than done."

She gives me a look that's all sassy.

"I don't see you with a man, Kez? What's your story then?"

"Oh, simple. I'm in love with a guy who doesn't even know I exist. He's off living his dream. End of." She wafts her hand as if she's dismissing her comment.

"Kez, that's kind of a big deal. You've never said anything before."

"We've not got to the mushy girl stuff in our relationship yet. But I'm super happy we have. I expect all the details about you and Owen. No holding back now. You've opened up to me, and I know that's taken a lot for you. Thank you."

"I'm sorry. There're a lot of reasons for that." My whisper is frail.

"And I've told you I'm a good listener." She tugs my hand getting my full attention and smiles.

I take a deep breath. This is the time—the opportunity—to share with Kez the reasons why I keep myself locked safely inside a box. Maybe she'll understand then. "Nearly four years ago I was… attacked. It was a stupid thing. I saw a puppy tied to the side of the road, all frail and skinny. I stopped to help him and untie him from the noose he had around his neck. They came up from behind me and dragged me into the woods."

"Ellie, we don't have to…" She takes my hand and looks at me with such sadness it nearly chokes the words that I'm finally ready to share.

"I know, but maybe I need to."

"Okay." Kez sits quietly, waiting for me to continue

"I was…" I close my eyes as I remember the first man

grabbing me with his filthy hands. How he held me down. "They took turns… with me. Used me as a punching bag. Tossed me around like some plaything. I was covered in blood and mud and… The minutes dragged on, and there was nothing but pain. I think I checked out for a while. My mind trying to protect me in the only way it could. Until they got bored with me. Left me."

"Ellie…" she squeezes my hand, giving me strength, but I don't miss the tears in her eyes.

"Anyway." I take a deep breath and get a handle on the thumping in my chest. It's not all the details, but perhaps she'll have more of an idea now. I can't look back at her. "That's why I have problems with people. With men. That's why I like to be alone, and why my anxiety effects me so much. It's what caused it."

"People would understand."

"No. It's taken me three years to open up to you. I trust you. I don't want people to know. I don't want their pity."

"They won't pity you, Ellie."

"Yes, they will," I state firmly.

The music changes song, and I realise Kez is waiting for me to say something. Or she doesn't know what to say to me anymore.

My eyes stare out of the window before I find the courage to stand.

"Ellie?" Kez stands next to me and throws her arms around me, engulfing me in a hug that crushes her body to me. "Thank you," she whispers. I can hear the emotion catch in her voice, and I avoid her eyes as I head straight for the door that will provide my escape.

I avoid Kez the next day. It's too soon for me to approach her after our heart to heart. Opening up did make me feel better though. Like a small part of my heart had eased with sharing my ordeal.

Another step forward.

All my work is up to date, and I find myself twiddling my thumbs by lunch.

It is an unusually sunny and mild day. I watch the sun glint off the calm waters while sipping my coffee. There are surfers out in the sea but no waves to catch.

I think about the sea kayak that I could try, while I bumble around the house putting the dishes away and loading the washing machine. Perhaps today, on a calm day, would be the right time to give it a go? I'd need Kez again. Maybe Alec could watch the shop? I google the place where I had my surf lesson and click on the sea kayak button. A three-hour accompanied lesson. I may be learning to push past some of my fears, but I'm not stupid enough just to hire a kayak and give it a go.

I phone and book in for the afternoon taster and make sure there's a spot for Kez as well. Seizing the day isn't something I've been living by. But that needs to change.

Snug. It's not exactly the word that I would use to describe myself, but I'm stuffed inside the kayak with my life jacket on, attempting to paddle out past the gently rolling waves. It's a hundred times better than surfing. Why in the world did I want to get thrown from the surf time and time again when I could cut through it in this mini boat?

The taster session is over before I wanted it to be, but that's okay. I'll be coming back. I want to be able to go out onto the surf and explore around the coastline on my own.

"What did you think?" I ask Kez as we start taking all the protective gear off on the beach.

"Yeah, it was okay. Maybe not my favourite pastime. But I don't even have to ask about it for you. You enjoyed it. I can see it in your eyes."

"I can see myself doing this, Kez. I'm alone. I get to be in control. I'm not reliant on other people, and I'm not being dunked in the water every wave."

Her face takes on a questioning look.

"Don't worry. You won't be expected to come with me to my next lesson. If I'm going to do this, which I am, I need to be able to work through the fact that my instructor is a man, but that nothing bad will happen. You'll know where I am." *It will be fine*. I say the last part in my head.

When I get back to the house, I'm exhausted. Mentally and physically, this afternoon took a lot out of me. George bundles himself onto my lap as I curl up on the sofa. My eyes begin to close when my phone vibrates to life, jolting me from my peaceful quiet.

I swipe my finger across the screen. "Hello."

"Well, you are taking my calls then. Nice of you to call your sister back." My sister's tone is all bitch.

"I'm sorry, Amy. I was out when you rang."

"Out? You've finally gotten over your little episode then."

I don't have the strength to deal with one of my sister's tantrums right now. More fool me for trying to be kind and send a gesture for her engagement. "What can I do for you, Amy?"

"Why aren't you coming to the wedding?"

"Excuse me? I didn't know you'd set a date. Mum rang to tell me you got engaged. Congratulations by the way."

"Well, Mum says you won't be my bridesmaid. You're my sister. This is my wedding."

"Yes. It might be for the best that you have one of your friends in that role, but I would never miss your day, Amy."

"You've missed a hell of a lot in the last few years, Ellie."

"I'm sorry, but this would be different." As I say the words, I can already feel the anxiety crawl over my skin, suffocating my thoughts. Hundreds of people. Strangers. Crammed in with no escape. Making polite chitchat and being expected to play a part. Thick bands of steel wind around my chest as I consider the inevitability of the day.

"Fine. I wish I could have the old Ellie back. She'd be there for me." Amy's words sting my eyes as I force back the tears that threaten. Maybe it's time to tell them? Make them understand what changed.

"I'm working on getting better, Amy." Although why should I have to defend myself to my own sister? Anger flashes through me for a split second.

"I'll keep you posted with the date. Don't let me down, Ellie."

"Did you like your gift?" In my head, I tell her just how much of a bitch she's being. But I don't.

"Very pretty, yes. Thank you. Speak soon." She hangs up before I can say anything more. I reach for the knot of metal at my throat and twist it in my fingers. Even if the necklace wasn't the hit I'd hope for with Amy, I did get my own present out of it. Plus, I made the effort to go and see Sylvia.

The effort for my sister didn't pay off, but it did for me.

FIFTEEN

The good weather of yesterday hasn't lasted. The heavens open and pelt the windows from the early hours of the morning, giving me something else to have a restless sleep over. Most of my mind is focussed on dinner tomorrow night. Or is it this evening now as it's past midnight?

By the actual morning, as in, getting up time, the rain hasn't let up. Swathes of water cascade down the window panes and the world outside is utterly drenched. The sea attacks the beach, kicking up a torrent of spray with each hit. It's a reminder of the beauty and ferocity of nature, which I find mesmerising.

The turn of mother nature distracts me from tonight.

The date.

Tonight feels… different. A milestone, perhaps. Owen and I have met a handful of times now, but there hasn't been a label on those meetings. Of course, there's a connection between us that is building. For me, anyway.

An evening date of food puts a romantic connotation on the evening, which I'm both excited and terrified of. But my heart will win out on this one. After all, there is a romantic in me somewhere, or I would never be able to fall in love with the hundreds of books I've read over the years.

The clouds rumble over the headland, washing the colour from everything around, and I sit and take it all in. An ointment for my soul. As the weather has killed any idea of going out, I indulge in a book, re-reading some of Owen's latest so we can discuss it at dinner. I pick up my Kindle with a smile on my face.

Doesn't look like the weather is on our side tonight. I'll pick you up at 7.

Owen's text brings a genuine smile to my face.

Looking forward to it. I'm re-reading some of my favourite book.

Oh really? Anything I might have read? ;-)

Maybe you've heard of her. Olivia Wren. A new author. The romance got me.

Rings a bell. What about the romance got you, Ellie?

I ponder Owen's question with a lump in my throat.

The honesty of it. The passion that Paul has locked away. How both Paul and Shelly have such a different view of love, but it's so intense you feel consumed by it as

you read.

As I write the text, I realise I want that. I want what Paul and Shelly have. Or what Paul finally finds in Owen's latest manuscript.

Do you think we could continue this conversation tonight? I want to watch your face light up when you talk about love.

My stomach summersaults at his words, and I feel giddy. Why can't I be this relaxed—this unguarded— when I'm with him?

See you in a few hours. We can talk more then.

I spend the rest of the day locked away inside my bubble of Owen Riggs' love stories, but it feels different now. It's like I'm on the inside and know a secret that no one else is aware of. I pour over Owen's words, absorbing them all. Once again, I think of what experiences he must have had to put such feeling into his words. Was there a woman in his life who overlooked him? The thought is painful, but I push it aside. This is fiction. It's not real life.

The studio is closed, so I can't meet Owen downstairs tonight. I message him to park outside and that I'll come down to him. The rain hasn't eased, and I shelter under the umbrella as best as I can before jumping inside Owen's car.

"Evening," Owen greets as I catch my breath.

"Hi." The nervous feeling in my stomach, which I've

been ignoring all afternoon, takes a dive, and I can't help but feel out of sorts. After the flirty conversation over text, I feel an expectation of what tonight might bring, and it's terrifying.

"Come on then. I don't know about you, but I'm starving." Owen starts up his Golf and takes the short but windy path heading out of Tregethworth.

The Blue Wave hotel perches on the side of a steep bank on the opposite side of the road. The original white-wash house has been extended extensively and is more glass than building now. It's stunning. Although, the weather doesn't do it justice. I've never paid the place much attention before, and now I wish I had. My outfit of smart jeans and a pretty top may be on the casual side for the restaurant.

Owen parks in the small car park and leaps from the car, rounding to my side and opening the door for me. He pulls me under his umbrella and puts his arm around me before ushering us inside. His simple gesture sets my pulse racing.

He takes my hand once we clear the front door and leads the way to a large, open-plan restaurant. It's the extended part, and the glass doesn't do a very good job of quieting the rain hammering down outside.

A waitress shows us to a table, and Owen pulls out my chair for me. He's looking smarter than I've ever seen him. He's swept his usually slightly messy hair back from his face, and a white shirt with the top button undone shows off his chest and shoulders well. Dark blue fitted jeans are the last thing I notice. He grins at me as if he knows what I'm doing. I fuss with a couple of my curls that won't stay behind my ears as my way of keeping my eyes from straying anymore.

"Wine?" he asks.

"Sure. Why not." I plan on giving my mind plenty of other things to dwell on tonight other than my memories of that night.

Owen orders a bottle of pinot grigio, and I set to choosing something to eat.

"I'm really glad you came out this evening. I know this is far beyond your comfort zone. The fact that you trust me enough is a huge compliment. Thank you." I look up from the menu, and Owen reaches across the table to take my hand.

"I do trust you. At least I'm working on trusting you." Everything in my body is telling me not to pull away, to go with this happy feeling that's growing brighter and stronger inside of me.

"I'll settle for that. As long as we can keep working on it."

I smile, not sure what else to say to him. "Your books…" I blurt, needing to change the subject to a more comfortable footing. "I mean, you've sent me the next Olivia one, so what have you been working on?" I'm not sure I'll be able to be as open as I was earlier with a screen between us, but I'm eager to hear more about Owen's projects.

"Well, I told you that I wrote before I came up with the Olivia stories, and I'm continuing that now."

"Oh, tell me more. I'd love to hear about that."

"It's not the same, Ellie." Owen looks away.

"Is it still a love story?"

"Yes, but—"

"Then I'd like to hear about it," I push on, hungry for the romance that's captivated me.

"It's a very dark story. There's no loving couple desperate to fall in love, nothing innocent. It's meant to be dark."

"Dark?" I question, not grasping what he means.

"The heroine is kidnapped, and she has to escape her captives. She has to find her inner strength. She's a journalist—"

Owen continues to talk, but I don't register the words. His face still fills my vision, and his mouth moves to form the words, but no sound comes out. Instead, the sound of laughter invades my ears. The cruel taunts and jeers that were the soundtrack to my torture. Moments pass and even Owen's face slips from my view. I see the blood and mud caked over my legs. The pain twists my gut as a wave of memories crush my previously hopeful mood.

How?

The cold air chills me to the bone and freezes me in place. My body seizes as my muscles turn weak. Just like they did back then when I couldn't escape. My legs failed me when I tried to run. My arms couldn't protect me from the fists and hands that punched and groped me.

Another twist of my stomach and I nearly double over, ready to vomit.

I close my eyes and breathe through my nose. In and out. In and out. The smell of wine and cooking brings me back to the present and my eyes open to a confused Owen. His eyes track mine, filled with questions.

I stand, knocking my chair back and startling everyone

else in the room. All eyes look to me, and an icy silence falls over the room. Owen stands as well, but I back away. I don't want to speak to him at the moment. My brain shuts down all the good that I've done the last few weeks, and lets the memories and fear from the attack take hold.

A shake of my head stops Owen where he is on the other side of the table. I clasp my jacket in my hand and turn to exit the way we came in. I can hear Owen calling after me, the fog in my mind slightly lifting. But I don't stop. His words mingle with my memories and distort everything I love about his words.

How could he write about something so harrowing, so awful?

I dash outside, and the rain cools my hasty retreat. I shove my arms in my coat and wrap them around me, seeking comfort of some kind. The splash of water as I stumble into a puddle drenches my leg, but my feet march on.

"Ellie! Wait!"

The shake of my head is the only answer I give.

"What happened?" Owen catches up with me, and I can't ignore him any longer.

"Nothing. I just… I can't do this," I lie, unable to reveal the true reason for why I'm bailing.

"Yes, you can. Don't shut off. Talk to me. What changed?" I listen to his voice and focus on the sound. The deep timbre has helped provide a grounding when I've been with him before. But I can't get past the ugly visions he's brought back to the forefront of my mind.

"Your book. It's… I can't. Goodnight."

"If you think I'm going to let you walk home in this, you're mad. At least let me drive you home."

The rain has already soaked my hair. Fat drops run down my cheeks disguising the threat of tears that linger.

"No, thank you." He's only a few steps behind me. Close enough to know he's there, but without crowding me. It's not much, but it's what I need.

"Well, I guess we're both getting wet then." His voice holds a stubborn streak, which I don't even think to fight against.

The sound of the waves gets louder and louder as I head down the road back towards home. It's a balm to my ragged nerves.

"Ellie, please. Let me help you. I can see your body shivering from here."

"I'm… I need to be alone. I can't…" He needs to stop pushing me.

"It's bucketing down with rain." He takes my elbow, but instead of the instant connection that's coursed through me all the other times, I want to lash out like I wasn't able to when they took me. I rip my arm away from him and quicken my pace.

"Fine. But I'm seeing you home."

He leaves me to my dark thoughts for the rest of the trudge home. The water eats through my clothes and coats my skin. Trickles run down my back and legs sending a shiver through me that wracks my whole body.

He doesn't crowd me or force me to listen to him. Owen's a silent shadow ensuring my safe journey home. It's a complete juxtaposition to what he's writing about in this new book, and it twists in my mind. The closer I come to arriving home, the more I can see my utter overreaction.

As we come up to the garden gate, I turn and catch his eyes. Concern and worry hit me as I try to grasp hold of my split mind—— trapped in the past but fighting for a future. At that moment, I feel more lost than ever. Confused over my growing feelings towards Owen as my mind clouds with memories of the past.

The tears slip free and add to the water now dripping from my face. I shake my head and retreat, rushing up the steps and into my bubble of safety. George fusses over me, concerned, as usual, and I cling to him as the fear and dread that invaded my body ebbs from me.

George allows me to cling to him for comfort until I'm ready to move. His little whimpers are far from the physical contact that I'm sure Owen would grant if I only let him. Yet it's Owen's actions that sent me into a tailspin. His writing about such horrific and sadistic events isn't something I'll ever be able to read and enjoy. I lived through my personal hell that night, reading someone else's interpretation of how that might feel isn't something I can stand to do.

My instinct is to curl up in a ball and hide. Crawl under the covers and never come out. It's the same way I felt when I was recuperating in the hospital. I didn't want to be judged by anyone or see anyone.

Weak. That's how I felt, and it's how I feel now, even after all the progress I've made. My sopping clothes wrap me in ice, and George's poor little body isn't enough to keep me warm. I shed the clothes and do what my body tells me to.

When I'm safely wrapped inside my duvet, George joins me. My ever-present guard dog. Instead of letting the weariness of the evening pull me to sleep, my mind races.

It fills with my favourite parts of Owen's stories, like little films playing on my own personal cinema behind my eyes. It's fiction. Everything I see playing out is a story. Made up to whisk us away, inspire, or simply be enjoyed.

People choose to read a multitude of different stories. Just because Owen is writing about kidnapping doesn't mean he wants to do that. It's a story. A plot. Just like his romantic ones. It's fiction. I've lived through the stories crafted out and committed to paper over the past few years to escape the darkness that infests my mind. My reaction was defensive. Automatic.

Owen must think I'm mad.

The thought saddens me because before my crazy mind took over, I was excited to see Owen. He made a part of me want to live again, and as much as I'd like to think that I've made all the steps myself, he was the catalyst that set things in motion.

I reach for my phone on the bedside table and come up empty. My bag, abandoned as I walked in the door still holds my phone. An explanation is what Owen deserves, but I hope he can accept an apology. The reasons behind my crazy behaviour will take a lot longer to admit.

The soft grey comforter that rests at the end of the bed is draped around me as I waddle into the kitchen. There's no message on the home screen. The hopeful romantic part of me wanted to see if Owen might have checked in on me. That was also the stupid part of me. I stormed out in the middle of our date and marched home in the pouring rain. He should be running for the hills not messaging me.

My fingers pull up a new message but stall when I think of what to say. Sorry doesn't seem enough. We've always communicated best through email. That's where we first connected, so I bring up a different screen, but the same blankness descends.

I click the call button and close my eyes.

"Hello." His deep voice sounds huskier over the phone.

"Hi." My tongue feels dry against the roof of my mouth as I search for more words. "Um, I owe you an apology. For tonight and how I reacted. I'm sorry." I rush the words, shoving them out quickly before I lose my ability to speak.

Silence bleeds over the connection, and my heart skips up, nervous that I've offended him.

"Want to tell me what caused you to freak out?"

It's a logical question to ask, and one I know that I won't be able to avoid forever. Perhaps a little longer, though.

"You know that I have problems with being around lots of people. Men, especially."

"Go on," he encourages.

"Something happened in my past that means that I'm anxious about my surroundings." I knew Owen already had this information, but I couldn't quite bring myself to tell him that his new story was a major trigger for my trauma.

Another beat of silence had me clutching at the phone.

"We've been out before. I've been with you every step of the way. Something happened in that restaurant, Ellie." He wasn't accusing me. He was simply telling me that he was more observant than I'd hoped and could tell that something wasn't right. The romantic in me swooned, but the realist hated that I needed to divulge more to him. And I did. It wasn't fair. If I wanted to see where things could lead with Owen, I needed to start being honest with him.

"Your book. The new one you're writing now." I pause to channel all the courage I can to get this next part past my lips. "It triggered a memory for me. I was attacked. That's what causes me to be so cautious. So scared." My voice drops to an almost whisper as a tear slips free from my lashes.

Owen doesn't say anything for a while, but I'm not scared of the quiet now.

"I wish I was there with you, Ellie." The strain in his voice is clear for me to hear.

"Why?"

"So I could hold you. I've been careful not to be overly physical. I knew there was something that made you keep your distance. That kept you wary. I just didn't think it was something so violent. You do better when there's a connection between us, even if it's small."

He can't see my nod of agreement. The hands, arm in arm. All the little things he's done have added up to something so much more potent in my heart than I want to acknowledge. It feels like admitting a piece of my past to Owen has knocked down part of the wall that I'd built to protect myself.

"I owe you a dinner. My place tomorrow? Sunday roast, well, sort of," I blurt out.

"That sounds like a perfect idea. Are you sure? I won't mention the new book. We can stick purely to romance."

That earns a smile from me, even if he can't see it. "Umm-hmm." I might lose the courage that this conversation has released in me if I don't confirm it all now.

"Tell me what time and I'm there."

"Say six?"

"Perfect. I'll bring a bottle of something with me. Anything else?"

"No. Just you. That's all I need. I mean, that's all I need you to bring." I stumble through my slip, but my voice sings a little with anticipation. Hearing that Owen is looking forward to it helps boost my confidence and reassures me that my delirious behaviour hasn't frightened him off completely.

"I'll see you tomorrow then?"

"Tomorrow. Will you be okay tonight? If I've stirred up bad memories, I'd hate for you to be alone. And I know that sounds bad on my part. I meant perhaps you can call Kez?"

"I have George. He's my hero. I've had plenty of bad nights and usually just lock myself in my room with my Kindle. Reading about other people's happiness is my escapism, remember?"

"Yes, but I didn't know what you were escaping then. I'm less happy about it now."

"I'll be fine, Owen. I'm sorry about tonight. I really am. See you tomorrow." I don't want to hang up. What a stupid notion considering I was so nervous about talking to him.

"Tomorrow. Sleep well."

All my fears about opening up about my past disappear in front of me.

"You, too."

SIXTEEN

I expected to wake in the middle of the night in a cold sweat, surrounded by demons. But none came.

After seeing to George, I consult the fridge and work out what I need to get from the store to prepare something that resembles a roast dinner. It has been years since I cooked anything close to a full meal for anyone. Kez and I were a dab hand at ordering in, and if we did cook, it was limited to pasta or something equally easy.

The fridge doesn't have a magical joint of meat ready to cook, nor do I have more than a few carrots and some salad. My food shop is usually delivered to the studio each week. Essentials I get from the small part of Molly's that doubles as a general store.

It's only a fifteen-minute drive out to the main supermarket. The sooner I get there, the sooner I can get home. I've been there a handful of times and if I hurry it will still be early and hopefully, quiet.

Every muscle in my body is tense as I grab the trolley and push it through the entrance. I power-walk through the aisles picking up a variety of vegetables and other ingredients. I make sure I have fresh coffee and a few other luxuries that I've not thought about for a while. The temptation to buy everything frozen is there, but that feels like cheating. A big part of me offered this to make up for last night. I want to put the effort in for Owen.

Less then twenty minutes later, I'm out of the shop and on the way home. My shoulders finally come down from around my ears when I walk through the door, and George comes to investigate what's in the bags. "Nothing for you today, buddy. But you might get a treat later, okay?" He tries to stuff his head in the bag, but I stop him before he eats the chicken.

The next few hours I spend cleaning the house from top to bottom. I only have five rooms, so it doesn't take long, but I want to make sure the layer of dust on the window sills is gone. Sure, I kept things tidy, but it's amazing how I've neglected the little things, happier to distance myself from everything around me by sticking my head in a book.

I shake off the melancholy feeling and focus on my next task. Cooking.

By five, everything is on track. Potatoes and the chicken are in the oven and vegetables are peeled and in pans. But the kitchen now looks a mess, and I'm wearing a baggy shirt and leggings. I double check the timers, shove the dirty pans in the sink and run the water.

With the kitchen looking presentable again, I set to work on me. I jump in the shower and towel off in record time. Standing before my wardrobe, I pull out my nice jeans and a pretty top. It's still on the over-large size, but the material is light, and the wide boat-neckline slips off my shoulder just a touch. My mass of curls look like I've lost an argument with a hedge, so I finger comb to the best of my abilities and pin the mess into a top knot.

A glance in the mirror tells me I've achieved a relaxed, casual look. A quick lick of balm on my lips and that's me done, just as I hear George start to bark.

I'd focused all my attention on getting all the jobs finished for the evening that I'd been too distracted to think about having Owen here. In my home. Alone.

A storm that echoes the rain and wind outside unleashes its full force inside my belly. Dips and swirls as wild as the waves crash inside me, sending a funny sort of nausea through my body.

Deep breathing. I've never let a guy into my home since moving to Cornwall. No big deal.

I open the door, and the wind catches and pulls it wide open. A handsome, although wet, Owen stands on the top step.

"Come in, come in." He moves fast, getting out of the horizontal rain that's started to lash the house. George greets him but doesn't appreciate the drops of cold water raining on him. "Let me take your jacket." I go and hang it in the bathroom so it can drip happily out of the way. "There."

I smile at Owen who's put a bottle of wine on the table. His crisp shirt is a little damp around the collar, and the rain has flattened his usually messy hair. His eyes are warm and open, and every inch of him sets me on edge, but for all the right reasons.

"Food smells… um, good. Thank you for offering. Can I do anything to help?"

"Um, no, no." His enquiry snaps me into action, and I realise I've neglected the oven. I open the door and pull out the potatoes. I try and scrape them off the bottom of the roasting tray, but they're pretty welded. Crispy might have been a few minutes ago.

Owen comes up behind me, and I can feel his presence without him even touching me. "I like my potatoes… crunchy. Sure I can't help?" Humour lies behind his eyes.

"Could you check I've not ruined the chicken as well?" I nod over to the oven again.

"Nothing some gravy won't fix." He takes the pan and sets it on the surface next to the cremated potatoes.

"I still have the veg to cook." I turn the hob on and set the pans to boil. The timers still had a few minutes left on them, so clearly, I'd gone wrong somewhere along the line.

I catch Owen from the corner of my eye, opening the bottle he brought over. He looks in a couple of cupboards before he finds two wine glasses and pours.

"Here." He hands one to me, and he raises his to clink. "Cheers."

"Cheers," I breathe out, glad to take a small sip. This was not going according to plan.

Ten minutes later, I've rescued, carved, and served dinner, and Owen and I are sitting at the round table in the corner of the kitchen.

"Well, Ellie, I wasn't sure we'd get here. Thank you for the invitation." Owen's smile holds all the humour of his tone, and he tops up our glasses of wine.

"Honestly, dealing with dinner has been the distraction I need." I take a large gulp of wine and realise what I've said.

His eyes lock onto mine, and it's hard not to feel the heat flare in my body.

"Distraction?"

"Umm-hmm. From you. Here."

"I take it inviting people over isn't a regular occurrence."

"No. Apart from Kez, I think you're the only person who's been up here. I keep my life very private."

Owen doesn't say anything else but turns his attention to his meal. I'm pleased he doesn't follow up with another question, and takes a stab at the food, although the dry chicken and rock hard roast potatoes aren't the meal I'd hoped.

"Owen, I'm sorry. This is barely edible."

"No, we're good." He spears a potato with his fork before cracking it open with his knife. "Nothing to it." I can't help the burst of laughter that follows. It's ridiculous.

"How about I just order Chinese? I have the number on speed dial." His face can't hide how appealing that sounds, and I whisk the food away and straight into the bin.

Half a glass of wine later and the food on the way, Owen's wandered into the sitting room and is running his eyes over my small bookcase.

"None of the romance stories I know you love so much are here," he calls out. As I bring the bottle of wine and go to top his glass, he refuses. "No more for me as I'm driving."

"Right. Of course." I sit down and shove my hands under my legs to stop fidgeting. "And I'm a Kindle fan, remember. Easier than real books."

Owen continues to browse before he joins me, sitting back comfortably and crossing his leg at the ankle. He's calm, and I can't see any sign of nerves.

"Relax, Ellie." His arm stretches out along the back of the sofa, but not close enough to touch. My mind flashes with all the questions I've had stored for him. My mouth opens, and I blurt the first one before I can properly engage my brain.

"Have you ever been married?" I mentally slap my hands over my mouth. "I'm sorry, I shouldn't have asked. That came out much blunter than I intended."

"No, that's fine." He takes his time, and I edge myself towards him, so we're angled facing each other on the sofa.

With everything that's already happened tonight, I've not felt intimidated or afraid at any point, and the small chord of tension I've carried melts away.

"I came close, but no. No wife."

"Girlfriend?" I just can't stop myself, can I.

"Not at the moment." His eyes spark, and I see him drop his gaze from my eyes to my lips and back again. It's fast, but I don't miss it. The heat travelling over my chest and cheeks is proof. I tuck my feet up under me and angle myself towards him.

I nod my head to acknowledge his answer.

"What about you? I'm sure I already know the answer though."

"No husband and I don't have a boyfriend." My tone is even, and I'm pleased it doesn't give away any of the emotion that's building under the surface.

"But you're okay with me being here?"

"Yep." I barely manage not to pop the p at the end. I glance at my watch and hope the Chinese arrives soon. The crackle in the air between us has always been present, but in such close quarters, it feels heavier. Blanketing me in a comfort that I've forgotten even exists.

Owen's arm stretches further along the back of the sofa. It's so close I can lean my head to the side and rest it in his palm.

"Thank you for telling me about your past. I know it must have been hard to share that." Owen's mention of my attack sends a rod of steel through my spine, breaking me from the relaxed mood I'd started to fall into. I nod, hoping he won't push. I may have opened the way to my past, but I'm not ready to let him in yet.

I stand and move my wine glass back to the kitchen and check on George. He's fast asleep in his bed next to the door. My hands start to fuss, moving things about in the kitchen. Another form of distraction. Tonight isn't about my past; it's about finally looking to my future, and learning to be comfortable in my own skin. Something that I've not been for years.

"Hey, stop it." Gentle hands close around my wrists and still my hands. "I'm sorry. I won't mention it again." He's so close to me that his words tickle my ear. His arms enclose me in a careful embrace that sends my heartbeat skyrocketing. The flight reflex that usually kicks in, doesn't. Running isn't on my mind. The contact between us is all I can centre on.

George stirs from his bed and begins a rapid alarm by barking at the door. Through the glass, I see the silhouette of someone. I slip out of Owen's grasp and take hold of George before answering the door.

Two bags of Chinese are handed over, and I place them on the table as I go and fetch the cash. Owen is stroking George when I return to the delivery man, who's taken shelter in the kitchen from the rain.

"Keep the change."

"Thanks." He turns and exits with no further fuss.

My stomach rumbles in appreciation as the aromatic smells hit my nose. I peek into the bag and start to pull the different boxes out. Owen swiftly opens another cupboard in the kitchen and sets the plates ready for us to serve.

"Although a home cooked meal would have been nice, I've not had a good Chinese in ages."

"Table?" I nod to where we should be sitting eating my roast chicken.

"I'd rather we drop the formalities, and you relax. Where to do you normally eat with Kez? We can go out to be formal another night."

"The front room."

"Great." Owen takes his plate and goes back to the seat he chose earlier. I join him, feeling somewhat self-conscious, but brush it off and get comfortable. We both enjoy the food for a few minutes, the conversation taking second place to the hunger we're both suffering.

"So, have you heard from your sister at all?" Owen opens up the conversation.

"Yes. But, nothing has really changed. She's very much about her and the wedding at the moment."

"Have you decided to go?"

"I'll be there. I want to be there."

"Is there a but in there somewhere?" Owen holds my

gaze, scrutinising me and he's right.

"But, I'm already nervous about the whole day."

"Anything that could help with that?" He drops his attention back to his noodles and rice.

"My anxiety isn't something I can switch off." I don't want to find pity in his eyes. I want him to see me as more than a girl who's jailed by her past. He nods without meeting my eyes.

"And what makes you feel more comfortable?"

My answer is too personal to admit. Owen has settled my nerves more than I could have thought possible.

"Familiarity. If I know the situation, the place or the people I'm with, it helps. Small things can startle me or bring back a memory that will set me off."

"About the attack?"

"Yes." I load my fork and concentrate on the food. Having the conversation focused on me is far too much and a change in tactic is needed.

"Why did you move to Cornwall?" I ask, not wanting the attention on me.

He gives me a crooked smile, sets his clear plate on the floor by his feet and sits back on the sofa, giving me his full attention. "Why not?"

"That's not much of an answer. You could have chosen anywhere in the UK, the world, even."

"Okay. I didn't like the distractions back home. My family is… complicated. And I needed to be somewhere to focus on my writing. I've always loved Cornwall. The house was for sale when I was looking. The rest is history."

"Sounds like we have another thing in common."

"Family?"

"Yes. And this place. There's a certain amount of luck, maybe, or divine inspiration about moving here." It had felt like the right thing to do for me. As if Tregethworth made it easy for me to move in.

"And you?"

"Why did I move here?"

Owen nods expectantly. I can't refuse as I pressed him. "It was an area as opposite to London as I could get. Hardly any violent crime. Property is cheap. And there was something about it that made me decide this would be a good place. Plus the shop was the only business premises available with accommodation. Win-win all around."

"Seems there was something that neither of us could say no to about this place. Have you finished?" I don't track his words as I'm too busy getting lost in the warmth of his eyes.

"Sorry?" I squeak.

"Your plate?"

"Um, yeah. All done." He leans in closer to me, and for a split second, I consider leaning towards him. Before I act on impulse, he takes my plate and collects his, depositing them in the kitchen. He returns with a glass of wine which he hands to me, and what I assume is water in his glass.

He sits closer on the sofa and resumes his arm-stretch along the back towards me. His body language is an open book, and the romantic part of me wants to crawl over to him and feel just how good it will be to be wrapped in his arms.

"Tell me what you love about books?" Owen's question sparks a fire in my heart.

"You want a list?" I smile.

"Sure."

"I can… escape. I'm safe in the world the author creates for me. I can get swept up in the story. Lost in the characters. I experience things I'd never be able to in real life." My heart fills with joy as I think about the words he wrote. How invested I became with his story.

"In Two-Sided Love, were you happy with the ending?"

"Yes!" I turn to be fully facing him. "It was everything. The way Paul opened up to Shelly. Put it all on the line for her."

"You'd want that dedication, that commitment?" My blush is instantaneous and embarrassing. I hide my crimson cheeks and turn away from Owen. Of course it's what I want.

"That won't happen to me though. It's fiction."

"Why not?" Owen creeps closer to me.

"Because it can't. It's too much for me. It's safer this way."

I expect something more from him. To tell me I'm missing out or wasting my life, but he doesn't offer that opinion. He just watches me. Like he's studying me—figuring me out.

"Now I know what caused our interruption on Friday, I'd like to take you out again. It doesn't have to be fancy, but somewhere you're comfortable. Spoil you. A date."

"This isn't a date?" I ask, happy to play along.

"Well, it is. But as you know, I'm a romantic at heart, and I want to take you out properly. Some would have called it courting."

I can't help but giggle at his phrasing. "Really? You'd like to court me."

"Absolutely."

"I can't see why, but yes."

"I can think of plenty of reasons why." His hand reaches out to tuck a stray curl behind my ear, something he's beginning to make a habit of. "You're beautiful, sweet, intelligent, and share my passion for books. And romance."

"I'm like a jack-in-the-box around people, have lived like a recluse for years, and have no confidence," I counter, uncomfortable with so much praise coming from someone as handsome as Owen. My eyes are low, and I fight the urge to fiddle with my hands.

His hand trails down my jaw and tilts my face towards him. "You had an experience that has left you with consequences. Don't let it shut down your future."

"And you're in my future?" Is this what I need? Reassurance and belief that there could be something between Owen and me.

"I'd like that." His smile heats up the air around us. It's as if he's drawing me to him, our bodies align, and our eyes lock together. If I were reading this in a book, the hero would lean in and clasp the heroine and kiss her with a passion that burns all the fear and questions away.

As if he can see the scenario play out in my mind, Owen's hand slips to the nape of my neck setting a blanket of goose bumps over my skin. He catches my inhale of breath with his lips as he captures my mouth.

My hand seeks out his shoulder for balance as I dissolve into a puddle of hormones under him. His free hand moves to cradle my head as his mouth explores mine.

Each touch and slide of his lips burn through me,

shorting my mind, so all I can think about is him. As the seconds pass, his touch grows firmer, my lips surer as the kiss deepens. It's everything I'd ever want from a first kiss, worthy of any of the books filled with love and lust I've buried myself in.

Until I lean back and Owen's weight comes with me, and the passionate embrace turns into a cage. It's no longer Owen's lips, but some stranger, smearing me with his touch. I freeze as the memory invades, but Owen notices and pulls away immediately, offering me a warm smile filled with reassurance.

"I think…" I start, not sure what I should say.

"I think I better go." Owen stands and takes a moment to straighten down his jeans. I stand with him, now confused as to what happened between us and if I ruined everything.

"W… was… did I—"

"Stop. This isn't about you. It's my job to show you how to trust again. And that's not something that will happen in one night."

"Okay." My limbs melt as if all the tension has been sucked out and replaced with jelly. Owen rests his hands on my shoulders and rubs gently.

"I'm not going to rush this."

"This?" I can't look at him.

"Us. This. The courting." He tips my chin to re-capture my eyes. "I need to go. Now. Before I change my stupid mind." He presses his lips to my forehead, and I can hear the soulful breath he takes. "Goodnight."

He looks around the kitchen before heading to the bathroom to retrieve his jacket. "Goodnight, pal. You look after your mum for me." I peer around the door frame to see him talking to George, and my heart squeezes in my chest.

His glance back to me is far too brief before he heads out into the storm, leaving my emotions in turmoil.

SEVENTEEN

A single kiss.

But I couldn't sleep for replaying it over in my mind. Until my dreams turned dark as memories invaded like poison. No matter what I did, the evil from my past always cast me in shadow, turning anything good in my life sour.

Owen said and did everything right. He was the ultimate gentleman, despite my awful cooking. The more time I spent with him, the happier he made me, and I wasn't ashamed to admit that anymore. Kez would be proud of me.

My sleep is restless, filled with visions that morph into bad dreams, although not full-on nightmares. By the time my morning alarm call of George wakes me up, I feel like I've only snatched a handful of minutes through the night.

I reach for my phone and see a text from Owen.

Last night was great. When are you free for me to court you some more?

The smile that erupts is impossible to hold back.

Apart from a few appointments and some paperwork that I need to keep on top of, my diary is open.

So, coffee tomorrow and how about we try the bistro again? Friday?

Sounds good.

I roll out of bed and let George into the garden, setting the kettle to boil as I do.

My fingers itch to fill Kez in on the details. Something that also fills me with joy. Our friendship, looking at it now, has always been at arm's length. At least on my part. No longer.

I check the time and note that she'll be opening up the studio shortly. My body springs into action for the morning routine, eager to go down and fill Kez in.

Coffee or Tea? I've got news x

Ohh that sounds interesting. Coffee. Large, please.

Two large mugs of coffee in hand, I take the steps down to the studio with caution. The door creaks as I push it open, and a grinning, pink-haired Kerenza confronts me. She snatches one of the mugs from my hand and gives me a twirl.

"So, what do you think?" She fluffs her hair with her free hand, emphasising the colour.

"I think it's… new. And pretty." The pink is more of an

iridescent powder-pink at the ends, blending in with her light brown hair.

"Thanks."

Her hair colour changes regularly. Although, usually only between the more traditional brunette, blonde and red shades.

"So, that's my news. What's yours?"

I nod to the sofa, and we take our regular seats. Kez takes a large gulp of coffee and waits.

"Owen came over for dinner last night."

A splutter of coughs and gasps sees Kez bent over trying to keep the coffee from spraying all over the place.

"Excuse me. Say that again," she chokes.

"Owen. I invited him over for dinner. Seeing as our previous date ended rather abruptly. I didn't want him to get the wrong idea. My attempt at a roast chicken was disgraceful, so we ended up with emergency Chinese."

"Chinese without me? I should be offended." Her gentle nudge on my shoulder tells me she's teasing.

"It was—" Kez looks at me expectantly, and I can't hide my excitement. "Wonderful. He was the perfect gentleman."

"And? And?" Kez is nearly bouncing off the sofa in anticipation.

"We kissed." I smile and drink my coffee.

"No. Nope." She emphasises every letter. "You don't get to leave out the details this time. Spill."

"We kissed."

"Was it good? Tell me it was good."

Good isn't even in the same hemisphere as what I feel about our kiss. It was a perfect moment in time, foot-popping, swoon-worthy and utterly perfect. But I feel like a sixteen-year-old who just had her *first* kiss when I say it aloud in my head. "It was a great kiss. Passionate, but not too much. As I said, a perfect gentleman." My whole chest glows with satisfaction.

"I'm so happy for you. When are you seeing him again?"

"Tomorrow, for coffee. Then dinner at the bistro on Friday."

"Do you know what you're going to wear? Oh, I can help. I bet you've not been on a date for a while." She starts to rattle off ideas and plans, and I have to bring her back down to earth.

"Kez, Kez… calm down. I'll be fine, but I do know who to come to if I need any help. Thank you."

She leans in and gives me a supportive hug. She holds me until my muscles give out and relief fills me.

That afternoon, with the storm from the night before having passed, the waters are clear again. I have another trip out on the sea in my kayak, which I'm looking forward to. A piece of time carved out just for me and something positive in my life. It feels good.

With everything that's happened with Owen the last few days, clearing my mind is an excellent plan.

My arms burn as I dip the paddle and cut through the water, again and again, fighting to go in the right direction.

"You're doing great, Ellie. Keep it up." The instructor has us spending more time in the surf today, rather than gently gliding on the surface, and enjoying the new vista of the Cornish Bay.

The physical exertion tests my upper body strength. I've done little in the way of exercise other than running over the years, and my arms are feeling it. In the final half hour of the session, the instructor relents and allows me to enjoy some time simply floating on the sea, with only minor corrections of course needed.

The hard work doesn't dissuade me though, and I schedule another lesson for later in the week. I want to be confident on the water. Confidence is something that is lacking in other areas of my life, but I want to turn those around, too.

With only ten minutes before I'm due to meet Owen at Molly's, George starts barking at the door. My body freezes at the unexpected interruption. I don't want to be late to meet Owen. I finish fixing my hair in the messy knot and step gingerly into the kitchen until I can see through the back door. His profile is recognisable immediately, even through the frosty glass. My steps skip across the floor, and I swing the door open, happy to welcome him.

"I didn't think we were meeting here."

"No, but I thought I could walk you. We can take George out after?" Owen bends to greet his friend with a rub behind the ears.

"He'd love that. Are you sure you have time?"

"I do. Besides, that's not for you to worry over." He wags his eyebrows at me before leaning in to brush his lips against mine. "Ready?" He grins at me.

"Um, yeah." I fight my scattered brain into action.

We step out of the fenced garden and head down the

road to Molly's. Owen has my hand locked in his, and just like before, my steps feel lighter.

"Now, don't tell me. A latte?" Owen asks as we head into the shop.

"A caramel one, please?"

"Sweet tooth?"

"Umm, kind of."

"You got it." I head off to find a seat. As usual for this time of year, the shop is quiet. Just a few people in the coffee shop or the general store area at the back. The tourist season will hit a peak over Christmas again, but then we'll be quiet until April. Summer is the worst season for me. So many people out and about.

"Here we go." Owen delivers the coffee and takes the seat opposite me at the table.

"Tell me more about your family then, Miss Carter." He sips the piping hot liquid and waits.

"Not much to tell really. I've told you that Amy is getting married."

"That's all you have on your family?"

I pause, expecting to feel my nerves start to constrict at the prospect of sharing my personal details with Owen. But this seemed a safe topic.

"We used to be close. Weekend activities, meals together, regular phone calls. We all lived locally to one another. It was ideal." Thinking back, I didn't realise how lucky I was to have such love from my family all around me.

"What changed?"

"Me." Owen knows the basics of what happened. I can speak of it without admitting how badly it broke me. "My attack changed me."

"I don't understand." Lines of confusion cover Owen's face.

"I didn't tell them. I didn't want anyone to know. And when I moved without a *true* reason, they held it against me. They didn't understand what I was going through because I didn't want them to know."

Owen reaches for my hand and rubs his thumb over my knuckle. I look away and fiddle with the necklace at the hollow of my neck.

"I'm sorry you had to bear your pain alone."

"It's fine. Really. I did it for selfish reasons."

"Don't you think they would have supported you? It sounds like you had a close relationship."

"It, I… no. It's not their fault they didn't understand what was going on inside my head." Turns out family wasn't a safe topic of conversation. "What about you? Family?"

"Well, some. My parents both passed away. My dad died overseas. He was in the military. My mum died a few years ago now. She re-married and had my brother when I was eleven. I didn't take that very well and hated my stepdad. Joined the army after my A Levels to escape."

"You were in the army?" I pull back, trying to mesh the side of Owen I know to a guy who could pick up a gun and fight.

"Only for four years. I have no trouble with the idea of serving my country, just not in the military. I hated it. Mum got sick, and my brother was causing trouble, so I came home."

"Going from the army to writing romance. That's a

pretty wide jump."

"Not a lot of people know about it. And I did plenty in between. But, as I told you before, I am an eternal optimist, and I believe in love."

After the heavy conversation over coffee, I think we are both eager to get some fresh air.

George bolts for the beach as soon as he's free from the lead, stretching his legs out and digging in the sand.

"What else have you got planned for the week?" Owen enquires.

"I have to meet up with Kez and review our client list. I've been somewhat short-sighted when it's come to my business. A little paperwork, but nothing else too pressing. You?"

"Head down, keyboard out. I can't miss my slot with my editor, or she'll fire me."

"That sounds like you have it the wrong way around."

"No. She's a total bitch when it comes to my manuscript. She will tear it apart if needed. Lovely woman, and she's the best." He bends down to pick up the branch that George has dragged up the beach for us. Owen snaps it, transforming it into a more manageable stick for playing fetch.

As Owen and George play, my eyes flick over the headland and out to the horizon. I could stand and watch this view for hours. The shifting winds pulling the clouds across the sky, the endless roll of the sea with all the tiny movements from the tide chopping and changing.

The air is ladened with misty drizzle ready to coat every surface it touches. "As much as this is lovely, it's probably time to head back. It's going to rain any minute, and I'm hoping to have a date with you that doesn't involve rain." I add as much humour as I can, and Owen laughs.

He leans down and kisses my forehead before pulling me in against his body. Learning to accept the physical contact as comfort is paying off. I instinctively want to nestle closer to him.

"I like this, Ellie Carter. Thank you for listening to me when you could have shot me down and never spoken to me again. It was a shitty start, and you didn't have to give me a second chance."

"That makes two of us." I lean my head against his chest and breath him in.

"You don't have to walk me back though, head home."

"Nope, can't do." He squeezes my shoulder pulling me in even closer. I hide my mile-wide grin as I dip my head.

All too soon we're back and have to say goodbye.

"I'm going to go out on a limb here, and assume you'd like to pick me up on Friday," I tease.

"You got it. Seven okay?"

"Sure. I can't wait."

"Neither can I."

The rain starts to fill the air as we say goodbye.

"You better go. I'll see you Friday." I turn to climb the steps up to the door, but Owen's voice calls me back.

"Wait!"

I spin and slip on the damp surface. My stomach drops, but before I can register the pain from falling, I'm encased in strong arms and staring right into Owen's warm eyes.

"Careful, Miss Carter." He kisses me before I can

answer. His lips firm and controlling, leading the pace. My nerves dance around my body, and the fizzing in my stomach explodes. Owen might literally sweep me off my feet.

He slows the kiss, pulling away before it grows too heated, and places my feet firmly back on the ground.

"Until Friday."

I nod and watch him walk away, a little dazed. The fine mist dancing around me is barely noticeable as I'm still caught up in that kiss.

My mind skips ahead to the possibilities of our date in a couple of days. Even though Owen talked about courting and dating, there's a pull between us that only intensifies with every meeting—a pull that reminds me I'm still alive. A month ago, I'd have thought having any positive reaction to a man was an impossibility, but now, my chest is fit to burst with a mix of amazement, heated with passion.

I concentrate on not panicking over all the little things that my mind trips over. How I'll feel with more physicality, how Owen will react to my scars, will I freeze like I did the other night again?

There are far too many what if's floating around my head, and so I do the only thing that will quiet them. I've somewhat neglected my Kindle of late. Something I'm beginning to think of as a good thing. My existence, although I've been waking up and living every day, has barely been a life. For the first time since that night, I've wanted to stay in my life, rather than rush back to the characters I've been reading, and that's a huge step forward for me. It might not have been the easiest journey, but I feel I'm on the right track.

EIGHTEEN

I didn't want the night to end.

For the first time, the evening went… like a normal date. I didn't go into a panic attack, the food was good and the company even better.

"Do you want a coffee?" It's a way to extend having to say goodnight to Owen.

"Are you sure?"

"Yes. Come on. George will be happy to see you." I turn and force my shaking hands to steady as I unlock the house.

I hang my coat and bag up while George entertains his new best friend. As I come back into the kitchen, I look in the fridge to locate coffee I bought the other week at the supermarket. I grab the French press from the top shelf and put the kettle on. The tremble of my hands is still present, but keeping busy means I can hide it.

I turn around and walk straight into Owen's chest. The impact stops me in my tracks, and Owen tips my chin up to look at him. I'm surprised he can't feel the drum of my heart as it pounds against my rib cage. Every atom of my being screams at him to lean down and kiss me, to take my nerves and anxieties away, but he doesn't. His eyes hold mine as if he's searching my soul.

On my next breath, I reach for Owen and smash my lips into his. And it feels so invigorating to take something that I want. His surprise only lasts a second, and then he's pushing back, pressing his lips against mine. It's delicious, and an ache curls deep within my body as if it's waking up after a long rest.

My fingers tangle in Owen's hair, messing it up even more as our bodies push against each other. I could get lost in this kiss.

Owen dips and hooks his hands behind my knees before he lifts me and sets me down on the kitchen top. He works his body forward, splitting my legs around him and tugs me to the edge of the surface.

What was a passion-filled kiss, now holds a promise of more. Owen cradles my neck ensuring I can't escape. *As if I'd want to.* His other hand starts to wind down my back, pressing against my arse before his fingers work to reach skin under my top.

His touch scorches me, and I have to pull back to catch my breath. It's as if he's stolen all the air from my lungs and set my body on fire with no way to quench the flames.

"God, Ellie," he groans the words through kisses down my neck.

"Yes." I don't know if it's a plea or acknowledgement of what's happening between us, but it's all I can say.

His hands run up the side of my ribs before smoothing down my stomach. As he gets closer to the top of my jeans, I hold my breath. He'll be able to feel the puckered skin of my scar. The ugly scar that's a constant reminder of how used my body was when they left me.

"Don't freeze on me. I want you to stay in our moment. *This* moment."

But it's too late. A chill that's down to my bones douses the heat of my body like it lives in my marrow waiting to turn me to ice.

"I'm sorry," I mutter into his chest, not brave enough to look at his face.

"What was it?"

"Your… hand. On my scar."

"Scar? I didn't feel a scar." He pulls away from me to search my face. "Ellie, I want you to trust me so much that you know, down to your soul, that nothing bad will happen to you when you're with me." His eyes implore me to believe him.

"I do. That's how I feel." I look up at him so he can see the truth in my eyes. "In here, that's what I feel." I place my hand over my heart. "But my mind plays tricks on me. It's not you. It's always me."

"Will you tell me what happened?"

I pause for a moment, wondering if I'll ever be brave enough to let him know. "Maybe someday."

"Bad?"

I thought Owen might have put some of the pieces together by now. What he must be imagining can't be any worse than the truth.

"It took me six months to recover, and that was just the physical damage. I wonder if the mental ones will ever leave."

Owen wraps me in his arms, chasing the chill from my body and encasing me in the comfort that I'm now continually craving from him. "You're doing fine. We all have baggage of some kind in relationships. You could have a psycho ex-husband, a missing son or daughter, a criminal record. All sorts of things. This is yours, and I want to work through it with you."

I listen to his words and know he's right. I'm more determined than ever to put the past where it belongs and only look forward. Some things will need some more adjusting than others.

"So what's your baggage?" He's right at eye level with me, my legs wrapped around his waist still.

"Aside from not coming clean about who I am to get your attention?" Looking back, it was a pretty low thing to do. But I can see the romance behind it. Or my romantic heart chooses to see it that way now. "Yes."

"I told you about my brother being a tearaway. Apart from him, there's my… ex."

"Go on." My voice holds a tremor of concern at where this may go.

"She didn't agree we should be faithful to each other. Of course, she didn't tell me that until after I found out she was screwing around with a man named Trevor."

"I'm sorry. I can't quite fathom why anyone would want or need anyone more than you, but hey, what do I know." I smile, showing him how genuine I feel about this.

He rests his forehead against mine and brings us closer together. My little freeze episode now long forgotten.

"And I hate that name. Amy's fiancé shares it."

"I imagine him as Neville's Toad from Harry Potter."

"You've read Harry Potter?"

"Don't sound so surprised."

"Trevor the toad it is. And I'm sorry. This isn't how I wanted the night to end."

"As long as there is another night, I'm happy."

NINETEEN

The next couple of weeks see winter start to threaten the usually average Cornish climate. The days are even shorter than usual, and people are already talking about Christmas.

When I go out for a run, the knotted and gnarled trees play tricks on my mind. Their inky black arms reach out to catch me as I run past. Luckily, there's only one stretch which is lined with trees, and I can avoid that route.

All the colour drains from the vista when the sun hides behind the cover of clouds. The bracken and grass-covered fields and hills look dull and lifeless. The cold fills every nook and cranny, and the ocean grows angry.

I've been going out on the kayak as much as I can, but the last week has been impossible due to the swells. High tide and bad weather have created a volatile sea that only the hardiest of surfers still tackle.

We've cut the office hours in the winter months in the past, but now we have the studio as well, we've agreed to keep it a little flexible. Kez still does some basic office work and admin for me, although there's little of that at the moment. However, she's throwing herself into promoting the studio and getting it off the ground. We've had, or rather she's had, a number of online enquires from the social media stuff she's done. Her hair is back to a dark blond this week, the pink already gone and forgotten.

Owen and I have settled into a comfortable pattern of meeting for coffee, text messages or emails, and eating together a couple of times a week. After the passionate burn out of our last date, he seems to have backed off with any physical contact and is letting me grow more settled.

It's the most frustrating thing in the world, and for once, it's me that's longing for things to heat up. He's attentive, considerate, and wonderful. And all I can think about is getting him into bed and feeling his body against mine. It's the complete reverse of a few weeks ago, but I felt how hot we burned with just a simple kiss and skin-on-skin contact. That taste gave me something to hope for, and now that's what I want. It's a big step in the right direction of finally moving on from my past. Even a few weeks ago, the concept of being physical with someone was unfathomable. With Owen, it's different because I trust him.

When I'm on my own, I still grow uneasy, especially if there's no one else around, but I'm learning to overcome and fight it.

Despite the change in weather I still need to get out of the house with George, and my runs are the best way to accomplish that. Owen even wants to join in, and it isn't something I mind, although a part of me still wants to ensure I have space and freedom without living in his pocket.

I set the pace with George just out in front.

"I was thinking. When I get this first draft complete, we could celebrate?"

It's the first time he's mentioned the book he's writing since my freak out over dinner.

"Sure." The run disguises my short reply.

"Great. I'm thinking next weekend, maybe?"

I nod.

He leaves the conversation topic, and we continue the one foot in front of the other routine for the next two miles. We wind down by walking along the shore, back towards Molly's.

Owen's hand finds mine and tightly squeezes as we listen to the roar of the waves blasting the sand. The force of the sea echoes around the bay, drowning out the seagulls and any other noise.

"So you said you were busy this afternoon?"

"Not anymore. Plans got cancelled." There's no way I'll be able to go out on the sea in this.

"Are you going to tell me what you've been doing these last few weeks?"

He pulls me against him in a playful way.

"It's a new hobby."

"I thought your only hobby was reading."

"Not anymore." And it feels really great to be able to admit that.

"Can you do it with a friend?" he asks, but I already know I want to keep this as something I do alone. My reward and my accomplishment.

"You can, but I won't." Kayaking is something to heal me. I can't have Owen encroach on everything in my life.

"Understood. But will you tell me what it is?"

"Sea kayaking." I hear the edge of pride in my voice.

"Really?"

"Yes."

Owen looks out to the sea and back to me. "Isn't that a little dangerous. I mean, look at the waves."

"Hence why today I'm not going. And it's no more dangerous than surfing or any other sport on the water. It's calming actually."

"Point taken. I'm glad you enjoy it."

"I do." My smile is broad and honest.

"How would you feel about coming to my house on Friday? I can cook."

I jolt to a stop. We've kept things to my house or public places so far. If I were to go to Owen's, I'd truly be on my own with him. Doubt tickles the edges of my mind, but I push it away. I trust Owen. Nothing bad will happen to me when we're together. My only worry about being on my own with him should be if I've forgotten to brush my teeth before visiting.

"Sure. I'd like that. You'll have to let me know where you live."

"It's nothing much. It's somewhat isolated."

The word isolated has me sucking in a breath, but I know it's an automatic response and one I need to learn to calm. "What time?"

"Whenever you want to come over. I'll be aiming for seven-ish for food. Nothing fancy, just pasta. Okay?"

"Sounds great."

Happiness isn't something I'd contemplated finding after the last few years. I'd settled with being content with my life the way it was. Functioning. Limited contact. Surviving.

But now I've opened myself up to the possibility that I could have more, I wanted to grab it with both hands.

Kez, I need help. Date at Owen's. What do I wear?

I send the text and smile. I have plenty of jean and top combos that would be more than sufficient for dinner in, but having Kez come on this journey with me is important. She's been like a sister to me. Plus she'll love being asked to help. Who was I to deny her that?

Are you in? I'll be around in a jiffy. I just need to grab some things for you. :-)

It's only just past two in the afternoon, so I know we'll have plenty of time. But I shower, shave my legs and coat myself in the only body lotion I own. Sexy underwear is out of the question as I don't own any. Comfortably feminine was the best I could do.

George starts to make a racket as I smooth the serum the hairdresser lectured me about, into my hair. I pull the dressing gown around me and go grab the door. Kez nearly falls into the kitchen, her arms ladened with shoes and garment bags. She has the most satisfied smile on her face. My chest swells, and I know that this girl is worth her weight in gold.

"Okay, Kez. You did hear me say dinner at his place,

right?"

"Yes, yes, but we need to make the right impression."

"The only impression I'll be making in those heels—" I point to a pair of black patent stiletto heels, "is that I borrowed my wardrobe from a stripper."

"Don't exaggerate, woman. I needed to show you options."

"Anything that's more my style?"

"Yes. Here." She drops half the items on the kitchen table and takes the others through to the bedroom.

Scattered over my bed is a rainbow of colour. Dresses, tops, skirts in all of the bright colours I usually see Kez in, cover my grey duvet. "Kez, this isn't really what I was—"

"Don't spoil it. I've wanted to inject some colour into your wardrobe in forever. You've got to let me now."

I pick the hem of a bright red dress that I'd struggle to move in and look at her with shocked eyes.

"Relax. Look." She rustles amongst the garments and pulls a pastel yellow shirt with an orchid print covering it. It's not too much and would team with some dark jeans well.

"Okay, nice. Thank you."

"And you can wear a skirt."

"No skirts. I'm fine. One step at a time, Kez."

"Spoilsport." She hugs me before flapping her hands at me to usher me into changing.

"Oh, and there is one more thing, but if it's a problem, just say. It's not an issue."

"Just ask."

I huff out and push the words out. "Will you take George for the night? You know. Just in case things go that way."

"Of course, you don't have to—Wait. You haven't slept with him yet?" Her eyes grow wide from the shock.

"No, and there is nothing wrong with that. But I don't want George to be here alone if things do happen." I turn away from her and go to find my nice jeans from the wardrobe.

"And you want them to, right?" She sits down, squashing the clothes she came over with, but not seeming to care.

"Well, yes. Of course. I do. We do." My words get stuck in my throat. "Yes." I turn and smile and hope the nerves that have invaded my chest are less noticeable when I'm with Owen.

"That's a great thing, Ellie. Ooo, I'm so happy for you." The little squeak she gives makes me giggle, and the pitter-patter of her small handclap rounds off the mutual celebration.

My phone buzzing on the side table distracts me from Kez. I peek at the screen and see it's Amy. I mentally roll my eyes, not wanting any of her negativity to bring me down before tonight.

"Hello, Amy." The warmth I project isn't entirely false.

"Oh, yey, you answer today. So there's been some changes to the plans for the wedding."

"Okay. That's great." She hasn't filled me in on any of the plans so far. She's only insisted that I attend.

"Are you sitting down? You need to be. We're having a Christmas wedding."

It was mid-November. That's a pretty short turn-around time for a wedding.

"Wow. That's fast. How come?"

"It doesn't matter, but you need to make sure you don't have plans the week before Christmas. I told Mum that we didn't need to worry as you never make plans, but she seemed insistent. So yeah. You'll be coming home for Christmas, Sis."

My mind swims with questions, and my heart picks up at the sudden change of the event that I'll have to cope with being only a matter of weeks away.

"I'll um… need a dress," I murmur, and I see Kez pick her ears up.

"They do tend to be the correct attire for a wedding. No dark colours though. You'll be getting your invite in the post soon."

She rings off leaving me somewhat speechless.

"Trouble?" Kez enquires gently.

"Just my sister. I want her to be happy. I do. But I can't reconcile the woman I know now and the relationship we used to have. She's turned into a real bitch."

"You shut her out. Your decisions don't make sense to her, and she's probably punishing you for them."

"Whose side are you on?" I jest, but there's a shred of pain that Kez would side with my sister.

"Yours. But I've only known the Cornwall you. I don't know what you were like before. I'm guessing you've made some big adjustments."

I nod. "This isn't the mood I was hoping for before going to see Owen. And will you help me again with a dress for the wedding." I look around the room to see if anything she had would be suitable.

"Of course. Now, forget about the wedding. You're going to go and have sex with Owen."

"Kerenza!" I all but snort.

"What? It's true."

And she was right. I did want to be with Owen. I'd gone there in my mind over and over since our kitchen fumble. There was a physical ache in my chest when he left. Keeping things simple was growing harder and harder, and the fear of my past no longer outweighed my will to do this. That was what had changed. I'd never wanted something more than the pain and worry I'd need to go through to get it. With Owen, everything was different.

The directions Owen sent lead me along a winding path off of the main road through Tregethworth. The route heads towards the deep harbour, around the bay, but the turning I need takes me up into a valley. Owen's house nestles into the craggy rock surrounded by foliage. The rain and lack of light make it hard to make out anything around, other than the make-shift track to his house. The white-wash cottage is traditional. The slate roof gleams in the rain against my headlights as if it's just been polished. The view down the valley to the mouth of the harbour must be stunning in daylight.

I park my car in the small space past the fence and turn off the engine. It's completely deserted. No neighbours, no houses close by. The nearest homes are the small cluster at the entrance to the valley. The rain makes a rhythmic drumming on the roof of the car, and the torrent of water trickling off the windscreen obscures my vision, now it's not being cleared.

Even though I'm early, it's pitch black. The dusk doesn't hold the light for long in winter. Despite the rain, I can't help but imagine the sun lifting the colours on the cliff face and turning the view into a vista you'd lose hours to.

A knock at my window makes me jump out of my skin. My hand is on the key, ready to start the engine, the other braced against the cool window. Owen stands outside with an umbrella over his head.

"I thought you might appreciate staying dry," he calls through the car window. My heart melts a little more for this man, standing in the rain, waiting to escort me inside. My hand pulls the keys free, and I crack the door, sneaking out to stand next to Owen. I wrap my arms around him, keeping as close and dry as possible.

"Hi," I utter my welcome against his chest.

"Hello, beautiful. Let's get you inside."

His lips are warm against my skin as he plants a kiss on my forehead and steers us from the car around the entrance to the house. We walk into an airy, open plan arrangement. The kitchen area to my left is all stainless steel and screams efficiency. To the right, in one corner, there are two comfortable looking sofas positioned around a log burning fire. A dining room table, already laid, is next to them. I'm drawn in by the warmth and the crackle and pop of the fire. I look around and catch my own reflection in all the glass. The far end of the house is completely glazed. The sitting and dining area both share views down the valley.

"This is gorgeous, Owen."

"Thank you. It's not much, but it is mine."

"Where do you write?" I look around to try and find space for an office or somewhere he has a computer.

"At the table. My laptop and books are hidden away in the dresser. They usually stay out on the table."

I nod and take it all in.

"Bedroom and bathroom are through there." He points to a doorway that breaks part of the kitchen up. He steps closer to me, closing the distance I'd subconsciously put between us. "Here." He peels my coat from my arms, and I catch him smiling.

"What is it?"

"It's nice to have you here. And you look beautiful."

"Thank you." I gravitate towards the fire. "Is there anything I can do? I want to help. That's why I'm early." My words run into each other as I'm keen to explain.

"Ellie, you are welcome anytime. And no. Sit and relax. What would you like to drink?"

"I'm driving, so a soft drink please." *Although I'd really love a jug of wine right now. Screw the nightmares.*

Owen comes back and hands me the glass, a bottle of beer in his hands. "Cheers." We clink, and I watch him bring the bottle to his lips taking a long draw from the neck. In the back of my head, there's a voice telling me it's rude to stare. But I can't stop myself.

I fight my eyes away from Owen and sip my juice, casting my eyes around the room and avoiding his contact. My nerves are like pinballs firing all over my body.

"Are you sure there isn't anything I can do to help?"

"No." He leans in, all casual and relaxed. He picks the glass from my hands and sets it down on the coffee table.

"I want you to chill out and enjoy yourself, so perhaps if we get this out of the way?"

My eyes widen, thinking he's talking about sex. All the blood in my body rushes to my face to burn my cheeks, but Owen simply cups my jaw and tilts my head, so he has easy access to my mouth.

Our lips fuse, and I sigh my appreciation. Everything apart from Owen is relegated to background noise as I relish in his affections. My arms stretch around to feel his broad shoulders against my touch. I dig my fingers in as I run them along the plane of his back and up to his neck.

The low growl from him sends a shiver of pleasure through my body, and I inch myself closer. He helps, pulling me against his front and deepening the kiss. *God, he can kiss.*

Heat radiates from where our lips touch, cascading over my body and melting the tension from my limbs. Owen is all around me. His fresh aqua smell keeps me grounded while his touch sets me free.

Everywhere we touch, burns. His hands blaze a trail over my thin shirt, and I long to feel his fingers on my skin. I wrestle with his shirt and finally win, gaining access under the layers of clothes and running my hand up his muscled back.

"Ellie…" I can't decide if it's a plea or a benediction.

I don't answer and keep exploring his mouth with my tongue. Every dormant sexual cell in my body is suddenly awake and catching up on lost time.

"Ellie, you're killing me."

"You want me to stop?" Insecurity taints my words, and

we rest our foreheads together.

"Hell, no. But this isn't necessarily what I had planned."

I kiss along his jaw and love the course stubble rubbing against my lips. Owen might not have had sex on his mind for tonight, but I did. I came with this on my mind and just because we hadn't reached the dinner part of the evening didn't mean we couldn't skip to the dessert.

I press my body against Owen's, and there's no mistaking the hard length behind his jeans. He groans as I move against him, locking my lips with his.

"Stop, please. I want to do this right. I'm not going to fuck you on the sofa. At least not tonight. God, I deserve a medal." The word fuck makes my body tremble with lust.

Owen talks into my neck as he nips and bites my flesh. Each time a pulse of desire runs through my veins, giving me a confidence I've not felt in years.

I stop and stare into his eyes, now ablaze with raw passion. "I want you, Owen. I don't want to be frightened anymore. Take it away. Take me away."

He remains utterly motionless for a moment. Time stands stills as we drift in our own private bubble. My heart thumps against my sternum as I wait for his response.

Owen scoops me from the seat and carries me across the room and into his bedroom. I don't have the time or the inclination to take note of the room. All I register is how huge the bed is.

He lays me out and rests over me. The heat behind his eyes, a simmer now we've both taken a minute.

"We don't have to do this tonight. We can take it as slow as you want. There is no way in hell I'm rushing things with you—" I cut him off with a kiss, not wanting him to remind me of the nervous, scared girl I've been. I want Owen to see me as sexy and confident. Not a victim or someone who needs to be wrapped in cotton wool.

"Please… I want this."

He groans, and I take it as his agreement that we don't need to wait.

His hand trails from my hip, over my stomach and to the top of my blouse where he begins to slide each button free. I lie motionless as butterflies are set loose in my stomach waiting for his touch.

When he reaches the last few buttons my breathing hitches, knowing that he's going to reveal some of my scars. The air burns in my lungs, screaming to be released as I wait for his eyes to settle on the ugly marks.

This is my first test. If I can fight the voices in my head that have beaten me down over the last few years and convinced me that hiding is the best bet, then the rest of the night will be easier.

My eyes don't leave Owen's as I watch him watching me. The heat and desire I saw earlier only grow hotter. He doesn't stop or even pause as he lets the sides of the blouse fall apart. His hand immediately runs from my belly button up between my breasts.

The air in my lungs puffs out, and I gasp for more. "You're so beautiful, Ellie."

I hear the words, and when I'm with Owen, I believe them. He sees me. The me I want to be, not the one buried under shame and guilt.

"Kiss me again," I beg.

He doesn't make me wait, covering my mouth and demanding all my attention. Our hands are a tangle of eagerness, fighting for skin. Owen tears his T-shirt off, and my eyes pop open as I admire his body. Wide shoulders corded with muscle set the picture. Defined pecs lead to tight abs and a dusting of hair at his navel. It's a sight I want to get used to.

"Had your fill?" he quips.

"For now."

"Good. My turn." He pulls my shirt off and moves to remove my jeans.

A few tugs and pulls later and we are pressed skin to skin, Owen's muscular chest is plastered over me. It's a delicious place to be.

As Owen's mouth sets to plunder my lips, his hand roams down to my knee, pulling my leg up and over his hip. The position forces his hard length into my thigh, and I score my nails into his back in response. The hiss through his teeth is the most erotic sound he's made.

"Ellie, I'm trying to show you I'm a gentleman. But you sure are making it hard for me."

I bury my head in his neck and whisper in his ear. "And I thought that was the point. You being hard." I tilt my pelvis to make my point.

His grin is suddenly sexy and dangerous all at once. He pushes up from me and stares down at my body. His fingers hook around the top of my knickers, and he slowly pulls them down my legs. I help, by lifting my legs and force my eyes to stay on Owen's chest. A good distraction from what he's looking at.

I see the moment he notices. His brow furrows just a touch, and I know I don't want to explain the small round scars on the inside of my thighs. My hands get to work on removing Owen's boxers and his erection springs free of the fabric as I slip them down his thighs.

"Ellie, God, I want you."

"You can have me, Owen. Please." My legs inch apart, the need settling low in my stomach and overriding any other emotion crowding at the peripheral of my mind.

Owen drops to the side of me. His fingers ghost over my skin as he makes a path to the apex of my thighs. He presses further, testing my arousal and setting me right on the path to heaven.

His breathing grows laboured and matches my own as his finger explore my slick heat. As he pushes inside, my body relaxes and my back arches in passion, as if I need to be closer to him.

"You're so ready for me. That's such a fucking turn on."

"Then make love to me already." If he waits much longer, I'll explode.

Owen closes his eyes, slowing everything down. He rolls away, rummaging around, and then he's back in my line of vision rolling the condom on. He settles between my thighs and the ache at my core throbs so hard, I wrap my arms around Owen's neck and pull him down to me. He nudges into me before his hips flex and he pushes all the way inside, stealing all my breath as he does. Our moans match as he stills, giving me time to adjust.

There's no stab of pain, no tightness. Instead, my body hums with delight. The relief is stark, and my eyes sting as

I realise I can do this. Pleasure is what I feel. Not pain or shame. The tears threaten, but my will holds them back. This is a happy moment, overwhelmingly joyful.

After a few seconds, Owen pulls out before thrusting back in. Heat blooms across my skin and my mouth forms an O as I get lost in his rhythm. His hands travel up to my hands, and he clasps his around mine, tangling our fingers as I wrap my legs around his waist. The shift in position sends sparks around my body, and my skin turns damp.

My mind relaxes, and I succumb to Owen and what he's doing to me. It's everything I've wanted, and my heart swells with love for this man.

A flash of an image crosses my mind, but I shake it off. Owen's grip increases as his breathing labours. His eyes slide shut as he picks up the pace.

Another flash, and a flicker of the image swaps. The man over me isn't Owen anymore. The stale scent of alcohol and cigarettes fills my nose, and my heart freezes as my mind goes blank.

"Stay with me, Ellie. It's just you and me." I hear the words, but they sound distant like a bubble encases me.

I try to pull my wrists away from where they're trapped but I can't. There's resistance, which pumps my body full of adrenaline. My legs twist, and I start to shake. The air in my lungs burns as if a fire rages in my chest. I can't breathe, and panic invades my body like an attacking disease.

Owen's off me in an instant, but I still can't fill my lungs. I shuffle to the edge of the bed, dragging some of the covers with me, clinging to them with my hands until my knuckles are white. My eyes screw up tight, trying to hide from the visions of the different men who each took their turn with me.

Hands grip hold of me, pulling me back, but I can't let them have me again. I shrug them off and stumble forward. Hot tears, full of shame and devastation, coat my cheeks as I start to see through the fog.

"Ellie, baby. Wake up. It's Owen. You're safe."

I stare up into pools of concern as my mind clears. Owen kneels next to me, holding my shoulders as his eyes plead for understanding. My mind rewinds over the last few minutes, and it's all too obvious that I checked out, allowing the darkness to overtake.

Devastation hits me like a sledgehammer. More tears fall as I fumble for my clothes, desperate to hide behind a layer of armour but having to settle for fabric.

"Ellie, calm down. Let's talk. Let me help you?"

"I'm…" I can't even form words. I feel rattled to my core. Everything was perfect. I was winning. Yet still, my past found a way to ruin my happiness. They delivered more than pain and bruising that night. They handed down a life sentence that I can't escape from.

"I can't do this, Owen. I can't escape."

"Don't run. Don't shut me out. I said we'd do this together, and I meant every fucking word."

I shake my head, trying to rid the wretched feeling inside of me and needing to find my own form of recovery. I can't stay here. It was a mistake.

I want something with Owen so badly, but he deserves someone who doesn't see a ghost everytime he puts his hands on her. In the past few years, it hasn't gotten any better. I've learned to live with the haunting memories. I've accepted it, but now?

Without giving Owen the explanation he deserves I leave, dashing out into the wall of rain.

"Wait. Ellie, wait." His voice is panicked and has an edge I've not heard before.

The keys get tangled in my hand as I try to click the button that will grant me access to the car. It's only when I'm inside that I look back to see Owen. He's in his jeans, bare-chested, looking lost.

It breaks my heart.

But it will be better this way. I'm not ready to be in so deep with a man I could give my heart to. Have *given* my heart to.

TWENTY

I don't sleep for the rest of the night.

Echoes of laughter, jeers, and taunts drift in my head. Memories I've tried to bury, bubble to the surface and quash any idea I have about closing my eyes to rest. And when my mind finally gives me rest, my heart punches out a beat as if it's being a stroppy teenager and has decided against the decision my mind made regarding Owen.

Heart and head are of opposing decisions when it comes to this problem.

The house is empty without George. I miss him. I could have collected him from Kez, but then she'd ask questions, and I wasn't ready to answer them yet. Instead, I wrap my duvet around me as I stare out the window at the rain. The house is shrouded in darkness, so I can see out. The streaks of rain lashing the ground soothe a part of me that's ragged and harsh.

I keep to my spot until the silhouette of the landscape darkens on the horizon against the threatening light of morning. Tentatively, dawn approaches as if it knows it might not have a warm greeting from the world.

Yesterday, I'd imagined I might be waking up in Owen's bed. Or at least waking up after a good night together. Now I can see how foolish I was to think all of the anger, pain, and guilt I've been carrying would slip into the ether once I decided I wanted more from life. Wanted a relationship.

The day doesn't start with any great announcement. Time drains away as I stay watching out my window. My phone dies after a message from Kez saying she'll drop George back in a few hours. All I want to do is snuggle up with my pup and bury my life inside a good book. A book that doesn't contain Owen's words on a page that sink into my heart and won't leave. I can face reality and put my big girl pants on tomorrow.

I'm drawn from my vacant thoughts by the door and the soft cries of George.

"Hey, boy," I say as I open up and get a greeting as if I've been gone for a week. "Calm down. It was only one night."

"So? How did it go?" Kez's eyes are huge and filled with interest.

"Can we catch up tomorrow? I just want to go back to bed today."

"Ellie? Is everything alright?" Her concern brings a lump to my throat.

"Sure. I'm tired. That's all. Thank you for having George. I owe you one." I keep my voice as flat as possible as I struggle through my words, hoping I won't get the third degree.

As I look up to say goodbye, I see the disappointment

in Kez's eyes. We stay motionless for a moment, and I have the feeling that it doesn't matter how little I've told her, she knows. She knows it didn't go the way I wanted and that I've let fear get the better of me.

I hide my eyes and say something about seeing her tomorrow before turning and leading George into the other room. The heat from my tears stings my eyes as I let them fall from my face. All my feelings overwhelm me, churning me up like I'm caught in a riptide.

When I was recovering, my mind was set on escape and starting again. It was the single focus I had and something I strived for. Now, I feel lost. My purpose has shifted, and I'm conflicted over what the right thing to do is. Lost. I don't want to be haunted when I'm with him. I want our time to be just us.

The urge to check my phone and see if there's a message from Owen is like a boulder pressing on my chest, the pressure mounting and constricting me further and further. It's unfair to want anything else from Owen after the way I treated him, but it's there.

Ellie
I thought I'd resort to our first form of communication. It seemed to work and was always where we could be honest with each other.

I'm going to give you some time and space to think about what you want, and if you still want to have a relationship with me. Please don't take my staying away as a sign that I don't want things to work between us, as that is the furthest thing from the truth.

I've put a few pieces of your jigsaw together, but I don't think I have enough of them yet to know what happened to you. It's driven me crazy wondering who could hurt you so badly. I will never hurt you, Ellie, and if you don't trust me, then I haven't done my job, and if you'll let me, I'll work night and day to restore your trust in me.

If you haven't worked it out, I'm crazy about you. And if you're honest with yourself, I think you are about me. I don't want anything negative between us, so I'm giving you time and space. If you need something else, tell me, and I'll give that to you as well. Hell, I want to give you the whole damn world.

You know where I am.

Owen

It's the sweetest and hardest thing I've read from Owen.

And I want the world. I want the world with this man. All the sunshine, smiles, and laughter. The happiness and fond memories you look back on that make you feel nostalgic and loved.

But I have to fix myself. I need to. My life has been on pause for three years, and it's time to change that.

The sun rises and casts Tregethworth in watery sunlight. The rain may have given up for a while, but it will be back. Instead of my usual route of running around the headland, I choose to go into the village, around and down towards the deep harbour. I've never run that way. It's far too busy in the summer months, but it's quiet now. Plus, I choose to see it as a step towards getting better.

That's my goal now. To give myself back the life I've wasted, and be the woman I want to be for Owen.

George is at my side every step of the way, although he's more distracted than usual. The undulating ground of the route means I focus on my breathing and pace.

There isn't anyone I recognise out and about as I pass, but then who would I recognise? The streets are clear and quiet to my advantage. Near the harbour is a small trinket shop selling Cornish legend and Celtic-patterned goods. I'm surprised it's open on a Sunday. I tie George up outside and pop in. An elderly gentleman sits doing what looks to be a crossword, behind the desk. I scout the room to find something that will suffice as a peace offering to Kez. The choice is relatively limited, but it's more of a gesture than anything.

"Just this please." I hand over the pen with a pink fluffball on the end.

"Haven't seen you in here before." The old man only glances up from his crossword.

"No. I don't think I've been in before."

"Huh. You're the accountant, right?"

"Um, yes. How did you—"

"Tregethworth is a small place, lassy. We all look out for each other. Wondered how long it would take for you to venture out." Still, the gentleman doesn't look up. It's a good thing though. His words have unnerved me, and hearing them while looking him in the eye would freak me out even more.

"I'm not that good with people, Mr…"

"Jenks. But you can call me Arthur." With that, he stands and offers me his hand. We shake, and then he goes back to his crossword.

"Arthur, how much for the pen?"

"This reader was the star in 2009."

"Pardon me?"

"My four down. Four, seven. This reader was the star in 2009. Any ideas?"

"Any clues?" I have no idea if I'll be able to help. Sounds pretty cryptic.

"Ends in t. First letter k."

"What about books that made it big in 2009."

"Nope."

"Okay." I push a five-pound note across the desk, not wanting to be held to ransom over a crossword clue. "Oh, The Reader was a film. Maybe it won something?"

"Huh. Good-o. Don't be a stranger."

I take the pen and disappear from the shop, not wanting to disturb Arthur for the change.

George is all sniffs and licks when I come back out. "Shall we go and talk to Kez then? I'll take you with me for moral support. Deal? But you've got to be on my side, okay."

I've only been to Kez's house once or twice. Those times have been to pick her up on our way out. She still lives at home with her mum, but I knew she was saving for a place of her own. Her house is on the way back home, about ten minutes walk from the studio.

I knock on the door and wait. Kez finally arrives at the

door, and I smile, trying to make my visit look less out of the ordinary.

"Hey."

"Hey. What's up? Is everything okay?"

"Sure. I was running and thought I'd stop off. I wanted to talk to you and thought I should do it before I came up with an excuse not to. Here." I shove the pink pen into her hand and wait for a response.

"You didn't need to get me a pen, but I do love it. Did you get it from Arthur?"

"Yes. I popped in earlier. You know him?"

"He knows everyone. He's the centre of all gossip in Tregethworth. He's also on the local parish council. It's good you've been down to see him. You can officially be accepted now."

"I wasn't before?" I didn't realise that I wanted to feel accepted until there was a possibility I wouldn't be. This place is unique and gets under your skin before you realise it. Or even want it to.

"No, hun. You're a tourist. But, you're on the right track now. Look, I'm not even up yet. Mum's home. Why don't we meet for a coffee? I could do with the caffeine. You can change, and I can meet you there?"

"Okay. If you're sure."

"I want to keep up our more regular catch ups. I most definitely want to know what happened on Friday. I feel like we need to be sitting down."

"An hour?"

"Great."

Molly's is quiet, just the way I like it. A new lady is working behind the counter. Not that much younger than me but she looks nervous.

"Hey. My name is Ellie. Are you new?" I sound as awkward as I feel, but it's the effort that counts, right?

"Yes. I'm doing the Sunday shift for Molly. What can I get you? Oh, and I'm Aubree. But call me Bree."

"Pleased to meet you, Bree. I'll have a caramel latte please, plus a mocha. My friend Kerenza is joining me."

"Oh, Kez? Yes. I met her last weekend. She's lovely."

"Yes, she is."

I tap my card on the card machine and pick out my favourite chair by the window. I can't help my instinct to scan the area for threats. It's like it's hard-wired into my body to check, but the usual pounding of my heart has subsided. There's only one other couple in the shop that I recognise, but I can't place them.

My eyes pull towards the window and wonder if I might catch a glimpse of Owen. He seems to have an addiction to coffee. Of course, that's my romantic, wishful thinking heart talking. Not the rational brain of mine.

"Hello. Thanks for the coffee. Perfect." Kez swoops in and takes a spoon to the cream on top of her drink. "Umm. Chocolate and coffee. How did you know?"

"A lucky guess."

As we sit with our drinks, tension begins to buzz in the air between us. I'm nervous to confess the details of Friday evening, and Kez knows there's something up. It's a stalemate.

We both turn our attention to the drinks for a moment.

My mind lines up the words I want to say, how I rationalised everything and came to the conclusion I did. That would only work if emotions weren't involved though. Not an easy task as mine have been running full bore for days.

"I'm going to jump in here and say, whatever happened with Owen, you need to give yourself a break and not throw him away." She sits back in her chair and brings one of her knees up to rest her chin on.

"I don't want to throw Owen away. Far from it."

"Good. I thought you were upset because you'd broken up with him or something."

"Technically, we weren't really together. Or we were, we just hadn't labelled it yet. And he's giving me some space."

"Space? Why do you need space? You've had nothing but space for years." She spits the word space out as if it's done her harm.

"I'm not ready for Owen. I wish I were, but I need to fix *me* before I go into a relationship. There's too much that I've not dealt with and it's not fair on him."

Kez's face screws up in confusion. "And what does Owen think about this? Because I'd bet he's absolutely fine with you just the way you are. And if you asked him for help, he'd be right there holding your hand."

"How do you suddenly know so much about him?" I can't keep the defensiveness out of my voice.

"I've talked to him, and it's clear as day that he's head over heels for you."

"Kez, please. You know my past. It's hard to be with someone when ghosts start messing with your head." I don't know how to explain it to her so she'll understand.

"You've been so strong, Ellie. You've worked so hard. Don't throw it away because you're scared."

"Don't belittle me, Kerenza. You have no idea what it's like to have to relive the hell I've been through. Or how I can be perfectly happy and calm one minute and then, the next, not recognise the person I'm with because the nightmare has taken over. I didn't choose this. And it's not fair to Owen."

"So you're going to run and hide like you've done the last few years?"

"No. I'm working on my anxiety. I'm pushing myself, every day. But this isn't like the books I read. Things don't magically fix themselves so the hero can whisk the heroine off for a happy ever after. That's the fantasy world. What I'm talking about will take time and effort and will be painful. I want to have a future with Owen, but I can't when I'm like this. I'm broken." It's the truth, and I hold it together enough to get the words out.

"So what are you going to do? Because if you ask me, it's Owen who's the key to fixing this. Not you on your own again."

"This is something *I* need to do. I want to do this. It needs to come from *me*." Being a woman who relied on a man for everything isn't what I aspired to be. No matter what, I needed to be strong for myself.

"Just don't shut him out, or you might find he's not there when you've finally come to realise you need him." She stands and leaves without looking back. Kez has never been this opinionated in the past. She's been a well of support and encouragement. Never pushing me for more than I was willing to give. Her words have me dumbstruck, not to mention riddled with doubt.

The next few days are as tough as when I was getting ready to leave for Cornwall. I churned that decision over in my mind a hundred times. A thousand times. I've bottled all the shame and hate up for so long, I'm not sure how to let it out if I wanted to. I'm at another crossroads.

"What a mess, hey, buddy." I snuggle George against me as I flop back on the bed.

The one thing I do know I want to do is to get out on the water. It will be great when I can go out confidently on my own. If everything goes well today, I'll be deemed competent. Not that anything is stopping me from venturing out on my own already, but I needed to know what I was doing, for my own sanity.

My arm, free from George's weight, reaches for my phone. I pull up my email and re-read Owen's message for the hundredth time. I've started a response a dozen times, but I always back myself into a corner. When I try to explain my feelings, I end up giving more away than I should, and I'm back to questioning my logic. But then I remember the feeling of terror at being trapped under my attacker and the strike of fear that shot through me. And then the guilt at realising it was Owen. I can't go through that each time we're intimate, and I sure as hell don't want to put Owen through that.

Owen,
Thank you for understanding. You'll never truly know just how much that means to me. If you could take my memories and stop the nightmares, then

I'd have already asked, but I think that's something I have to fix for myself. I want to. And that's something you've done for me. You've made me want to be the woman you deserve, without the crazy baggage. Give me some time because I really want there to be an us.

Love Ellie.

I read the words back and picture what Owen will interpret from them. He's a master at putting emotion on the page. Will he feel my emotions, what I'm telling him in these words?

My finger hovers over the paper aeroplane sign on my phone ready to send, but something holds me back.

George chooses that moment to jump up from his comfortable slumber, jarring my body.

"George! Look what you made me do. You silly pup." My finger taps the icon. It's too late to call the email back. Owen has my words, and I have to hope they were the right thing to say.

I switch the phone off and roll over, determined to continue the day without letting it fall apart. The view from the window is calm. Stillness reigns over the beach with no one in sight. Even the sea is muted, with ripples instead of crashing waves. Perfect for me to go out and channel some inner peace.

TWENTY-ONE

The last lesson on the water is the best I've had. My instructor has signed me off, and I'm free to paddle on the waves on my own.

For the last few weeks, I've been taking advantage of my new freedom and any calm days, to come out here to spend time with no one but myself. Nothing new about that, but at the same time, everything has changed.

I've ignored nearly everything around me. Kez has run the shop, organised my dress for the wedding, dealt with Alec, and I've spent as much time out on my own as I dare.

The briny air fills my lungs, and, for the first time in forever, I feel proud of myself. I tip my head to the sky and slip my eyes closed. I'm happy—or at least my own brand of happy that I've found something for me that I love. Each day I've been out on the water, I've gained more confidence and paddled out further, content to be able to see a new perspective on the beach that I stare at every day.

A warmth that can't be from the sun, because it's absent as usual, infuses me. With my mind, I focus on the sensation and try to wrap myself around it and use it as a source of happiness. The harder I try to contain it, the more it slips away like a summer breeze through my fingers.

Owen and the events of the previous weeks invade my head. It was foolish to hope that he would be able to do something that I haven't been able to for three years—help leave my shadows in the past, but the heat and desire between us are as overpowering now as they were when we were together. Even the echo of his touch sends my heart into overdrive.

My memories twist and a flicker of the horror I endured cuts between the good visions of Owen. I shake my head and slap the water with my paddle before a deep, cathartic scream bubbles up from within me. I bellow my anger out at the sea until my lungs can't sustain it, and I drop forward, panting for air with tears streaming down my face.

As if mother nature heard my cry, heavy splashes of rain fall on my face, leaving me cold. Deep drops dance across the surface of the sea as the wind picks up. A deep grumble from the clouds that have gathered has me in a panic as I dip my oar into the water and turn around.

My arms reach and pull as hard as I can to propel me faster through the water. My hair sticks to me like a second skin, and my eyes have to scrunch up in order to see anything through the rain. My vision is masked by a wall of grey. The sea and sky merge into a never-ending canvas that I struggle to decipher. The cliffs are still on my left, so I know I'm heading in the right direction, but the calm and serene waters of an hour ago are now choppy and hard to navigate.

The soft noise of the rain hitting the water grows to a

dull roar in my ears as the rolling waves crashing into shore join in. Nature's orchestra builds as I begin to panic. Each arm burns as I dig through the water. With every dip of the blade into the sea, it's harder to cut through. My forward momentum slows, and I can feel the swell of the waves pushing me back.

I swipe the water from my eyes as my teeth grit down against each other. *I can do this.* The pressure of my fingers holding onto the oar turns my hands white. Either that or it's the icy water. The wetsuit that had previously kept me warm fails as a chill climbs up my spine and zaps my energy.

Movement pulls my attention from my path, and the swell of a wave engulfs me, dowsing me in frigid water. The sting of salt on my taste buds has me coughing as I spit the sea water out.

The next wave pulls me under, and the world disappears as I fight free of my kayak. My legs kick against the water to right myself as the burn of my lungs spreads through my chest. I gasp for air and swallow more salty water.

I force my eyes to focus so I can orientate myself. Getting to shore is my only goal, and I have to make it. I put the beach in my sights and kick forward as I'm hit by the crash of another wave, sending me under again. The noise is cancelled out, and I'm left holding my breath and praying for calm.

The cold bites against my skin as if a hundred needles are scratching against every inch of exposed skin. Taking a breath grows harder but more necessary as I swing my arms against the water, trying to paddle in.

A crack of thunder echoes around the beach as I fight

to keep my arms and legs moving. It can't be that much further. I blink and squint through salt-filled eyes and see I'm dangerously close to the rocks at one side of the bay. I'm way off course.

Water washes over my head, but I relax as much as possible and let the tide wash me in. My arms are jelly in the water, and the fear of not reaching shore pumps my heart and brain to work harder.

I flounder about in the water, desperate to sink my feet into the sand. The sea's up around my armpits, and I have no stability for when the next wave hits, pulling me under again. But I fight it. I fight the pull and force myself forward.

Owen. The thought of not seeing him, explaining my feelings, everything that's been hanging in the air spurs me on, and I'm left with the desperate need to see him again. To feel the comfort only he's been able to deliver. He's what I want and what I need.

My feet stumble and trip against the gritty floor, and I stagger forward onto my knees and crawl out of the water. My body shudders with cold, and my limbs ache as I collapse a few feet from the lapping waves. Salt and sea invade my airways as I fight to pull in the oxygen my body screams for. With every breath, the shakes grow more intense until my skin feels like it's burning from the cold.

With the little energy spike from the adrenalin, I twist my body onto my back and lie facing the sky. The rain pelts my face, but it stops me from getting a mouthful of wet sand.

"Hey! Are you alright?"

A voice registers somewhere inside my head, but I choose to ignore it. My entire body sinks deeper into my impression in the sand, and I welcome the heaviness that overtakes me.

"Ellie, baby, we need to get you somewhere dry."

This time the voice is closer and... familiar. Somewhere in the recess of my mind I know I can relax. But at the same time, there's a warning bell sounding. It's not loud enough to disturb me, but it's there.

The initial contact must have roused me.

"Not the place to take a nap. Come on, we need to get you warm and dry."

Strong arms lift my body up, and I'm aware of being moved. "No. No, please." My speech sounds distant and slurred, but alarm is piercing through the fog. My eyes open and a man with a hoody up over his head is moving me in his arms. My body wakes up, and I fight my automatic reaction to flee. It's what I want to do, what I've done for too long.

"Hey, hey, hey. Easy. Ellie, it's me, Owen. I'm not going to hurt you. You know that. Listen to my voice. Hear me. I need to get you inside."

"Owen?" I recognise his voice, and as my eyes adjust, I see it's him. "Home," I mutter behind trembling lips and chattering teeth. A sense of relief finally settling over me.

"You got it."

I nod. Before he starts to lead me up the beach, I look back for my kayak.

"Don't worry. I'll come back and pick it up."

"Tha tha thank... y yooo yoouu. I I..."

"Shhhh. Save your energy. Plenty of time to talk later."

Owen takes my weight as we start walking up the beach. Each step hurts as I lose more and more feeling in my feet and legs. My chest constricts on every pull of air into my lungs, screaming for relief, and my nose and throat begin to burn from the water I've ingested.

Each step, I think of the warmth of home and wish to everything in the world that I'll be able to get there and forget everything from the last couple of weeks and just enjoy being safe in Owen's arms.

"Down," I groan when we arrive at the bottom of the steps.

"I don't think so." Owen ignores my request and carries me up as if I weigh nothing. He places me on my shaky legs at the top. George barks loudly before we even reach the door, and I push it open and all but collapse into the kitchen.

"I think we should call an ambulance. Or I can take you to hospital to check you over."

That's the last thing I want. "No. Th th thaank yoouuu," I force out. As much as George wants to check I'm okay, I need to warm up. I fall onto the sofa and pull the throws over my soggy body and wrap up tight. After a few minutes, the shivering subsides, and I can breathe easier.

"No, Ellie, you need to get out of that wetsuit. Get you dry."

I don't listen and close my eyes as the cocoon of heat starts to build. My eyelids drop, and the energy to keep them open escapes me.

"Ellie!" Kez cries from the kitchen. "What the? What did you do?"

Her screech has me opening my eyes in a start. The memories flashback, and I struggle to look around. "Trouble.

Water. Cold." She'll have to be content with my mono word answers.

She pushes my legs out of the way and covers me in another layer of warmth and leans over me, rubbing my back through the blankets.

I'm vaguely aware of hushed conversation, but I'm too tired to stay tuned in, and I give in to the peace and darkness.

Noise from... somewhere pulls me from my slumber, and I blink my eyes open. A close up of the weave of the pillow fabric is out of focus, so I twist my head in the direction of the door. Kez is in the kitchen looking at her phone. Voices, not music, sounds, and I assume she's keeping herself from being bored. Owen sits at the small table next to her.

I stretch out and push the bubble of warmth from my body and resist shuddering at the change in temperature. My movement catches Kez's attention, and she whips up and comes to stand in front of me.

"Hey, you alright?" she takes my arm.

"Sure." I sound like I've just ended a four-day smoking binge.

"You need to get out of that suit and wash. You'll warm up and feel better."

"Agreed. You don't need to stay." I keep my eyes focused on Kez and resist looking at Owen.

"Shh. I am staying to make sure you're actually okay." My smile is weak, and I can feel the quiver in my cheeks.

The wetsuit is stuck tight to my skin. The salt and sand have conspired to make a glue that makes peeling my limbs out of the suit more than a chore. After wrestling the rubber material into submission, I dive under the hot water and drench myself in heat. A cloud of steam envelopes me, and I relax in the peacefulness of it.

The steady pour of water from the showerhead is the only noise. No rush of the water, no roar of the thunder overhead. Peace.

My body absorbs all the heat from the stream of water, replenishing it as if it were energy drained from my body. Time passes, and I let the water soothe me, taking away all the fear and panic from earlier. The murky water swirling around me is at the forefront of my mind. I stand up taller and force that image away. I've let my past haunt me for far too long. If I let it, this could turn into something else to worry over and prevent me from moving forward. Up until today, the sea has been a remedy. A way of me gaining back a part of me that was lost.

I turn the water off and wrap myself up in the largest towel in the hamper before pulling on my warmest pyjamas.

"Hey." My voice is still hoarse.

"Better?"

"Much. Thank you. Where's Owen?" I might have avoided his eyes before, but now I crave the comfort of his arms.

"He needed to go home and change. And sleep. He didn't want to leave you, but I told him I wouldn't be going anywhere."

"Oh, right. You don't have to stay. I promise I'm fine."

She comes over to me and wraps me in her arms. "Right. Now I've done that. I am so mad at you right now. What were you trying to prove?"

Her angry tone is a change that's hard to follow, and I cough on a gasp of breath.

"Prove? Nothing. What are you talking about?"

"Really? Who goes out on the water in that weather. You were being reckless. Proving you don't need anyone else in your life. That you can do it all on your own. Because that's what you've been doing—that's what you've been used to these few years." She kicks out her hip, and with her hands resting there, she looks all business.

"Slow down. That's not true, Kez. Can we do this another day?"

"No."

"Look, I've been out on the water plenty, but I didn't notice the change in the weather until it was too late. It was an accident. As for the rest, I'm learning to let people in."

"You have. But you know what? You need to work harder. You have people around you who care for you. You have a community waiting to make friends, and you hold everyone at arm's length for fear of something bad happening. Well, shit can happen every day. Yesterday just shows you that. You can choose to go off on your own, and you can still risk your life. No one else to blame but yourself."

"Are you finished?" My brows pop up at her outburst.

"No. I'm not. You've lived with your past haunting you for so long that you've accepted it. Well, I call bullshit. You're scared. Don't let that stop you from grabbing happiness with both hands. Owen cares for you." The verbal sparring is new for us.

"And what do you know about love or happiness?" Kerenza doesn't have the right to tell me how to run my life when she has no experience of what I'm dealing with.

"This isn't about me. Not today. You need to realise that bad stuff can happen every single day. You can't avoid it. I've seen how hard it is on you, but it's time to work towards you being happy. Talk to Owen. Talking helps. We're here to support you, Ellie. It's time you opened your eyes." Her voice softens, and a pleading replaces the anger that tells me how desperate she is for me to take heed of her advice.

"I have, Kez. This is what I want. But I can't click my fingers and pretend that everything is all right. Do you think I want to freeze each time Owen puts his hands on me, or get sucked into a flashback from which all I want to do is escape? It's not fair that my past still controls me. But for the first time, I want to fight it. Real life is hard, and I may not have been willing to work before this. But I am now. So don't lecture me."

Taking all her words is hard. Kez is usually such a carefree and bubbly person, but she sure can tear a strip off you when she wants. Everything she's said is the truth which makes the thrash of her tongue harder to hear.

It's ironic that the activity I've chosen to help build my confidence also put me in danger. I'd associated people with being a threat for so long that being on my own seemed the safest solution for every part of my life. And here I am, half drowned through my own behaviour.

Alone.

I thought that like everything else in my world, overcoming my past was something I had to do for myself.

Work through my nightmares and heal on my own. Perhaps not. When I was in danger of drowning, the first person I wanted to see was Owen. The man I wanted to seek comfort from was Owen.

"How did you know what happened, anyway?" I don't want to fight with Kez anymore.

"Owen. He was out walking and saw someone in trouble. He didn't realise it was you until he reached you on the sand. He called me after you got back."

It's on the tip of my tongue to say that I didn't need any help, but in this instance, I did. It was a close call that I even made it back to the beach.

"I need to thank him."

"He went back to get your kayak. It's under the steps in the garden. I think he was just relieved that you let him help. Do you want tea?" She turns away and fills the kettle, expecting my confirmation.

"Sure." I rummage in the cupboard to see if there's any honey hiding away, hoping it might soothe my throat.

"Will you talk to him?"

I take the steaming mug she hands me and stir a scoop of congealed honey into the water, watching as it dissolves to nothing. "Yes. He's not someone I want to let slip through my fingers. Being out there in the water, crawling onto the beach, he's where my mind went to."

"Then don't let your past hold you back anymore. Go and tell him how you feel. I guarantee that he'll be there for you." Kez made it sound so simple, and I wanted to believe her more than anything else in the world.

TWENTY-TWO

Kez didn't leave my side, even when I fell back to sleep on the sofa. With all the sleep I'd had, I was awake before dawn, feeling caged in my own home, waiting for the time to click around to morning.

The words run together on the screen as my eyes race to take them in. I know the words. I've read them before, and even with time and other stories in the way, it feels like he's inked his sentences into my soul.

This book changed me. It sounds such a silly thing to admit to out loud, but it did. And as I sit and absorb it all over again, I can see my life changing. If I want a life with Owen in it, I can't sit back and let time heal. Time doesn't heal all wounds. Time can cause them to fester and rot, let an infection take root and poison your blood. You have to take action against that. Something I've been neglectful about.

The invitation to Amy's wedding lies to the side in the kitchen. Beautifully embossed with a wax heart seal at the bottom. I haven't officially RSVP'd, but she knows I will be there. There's no choice if I don't want to alienate my family for the rest of my life. The romantic and hopeful part of my heart believes that I can mend the bridges that have crumbled in the last few years. An olive branch, perhaps. Although it's really a long shot at this point. Tomorrow, I'll find out. It's come around so soon. I should have invited Owen to come with me weeks ago. It's another item on my list of things I should have said to him before now.

The dawn light barely tinges the sky. It's calm outside. Just how yesterday had begun. The sobering thought spurs my body into action. Owen won't be awake this early. He's a night owl, not an early riser. But I can't wait any longer.

I jump in the car and make my way up to his place. This is too important to put off. A sliver of apprehension coils in my gut, but the words in his email stay focused in my mind.

My car delivers me to Owen's without incident. Shadow coats Owen's home and nothing but blackness comes from the windows. The early hour gives me pause, and I'm struck by déjà vu as I sit waiting in my car. This time, Owen won't be coming to meet me with an umbrella.

The pounding in my chest grows stronger as my nerves increase. My limbs feel like they've been tied down with string and don't want to cooperate. I force my mind to overpower the muscles, so I can head to the front door. There's no doorbell, so I rap my knuckles on the smooth wood, loud and firm. And wait.

And wait.

I take a deep breath, squaring my shoulders and standing straighter as I wait. The wind tunnels past, biting against my clothes and cooling my skin. The landscape is raw and wild but beautiful in its ruggedness.

As the seconds tick on, my anxiety grows to the point

I can feel myself vibrating with the need to flee. I raise my hand again and drum against the door.

"Alright, for fuck's sake. It's not even morning in my book." A gruff-sounding Owen swings the door open as he complains. Having a cup of coffee to thrust into his hand would have helped smooth this meeting.

He looks up through sleep-filled eyes, and I see the moment when recognition hits. His eyes widen, and he stands taller. He's wearing a pair of dark blue and green checked pyjama bottoms. Nothing covering his chest. My eyes dip from his and cast over his flesh and down his abs.

"Is everything okay?" He switches his annoyance to concern.

"Fine. Sort of. Nothing bad. I hope," I stumble through my words, hoping he'll invite me in, so I don't have to wait in the cold any longer.

"Okay." He pushes the door wider and walks back inside without another word. His behaviour sends a shiver of apprehension through me. What if I've imagined more to us than there is? Have I taken the words from his story and imagined myself as the heroine—blowing this relationship into a potential epic love, just like in his book.

Owen stalks to the kitchen where he pulls out a couple of mugs and puts them on the side. Dishes fill the sink, and as I look around, the house is anything but the tidy and sleek home I visited the first time.

"Coffee?" He doesn't turn to ask me but continues with his preparations.

"Please. I'll just take a seat." There's no fire crackling away today. The whole room has a gloomy feel compared to the warmth of the first night I visited. Papers cover the table he uses as a desk, along with books and his computer. A whirring mechanical noise comes from the kitchen, and I see a coffee pod machine on the side.

He brings two mugs over and sits them on the table in front of us. His hands rub over his face as if he's still waking up. I take the time to admire him, and as I do, the anxiety that had filtered through me from Owen's welcome melts. Being in his presence soothes something within me—a part of me that's been on constant alert for the last three years. This man is who I want at my side to help me fight my demons. He's been the only person aside from Kez who I've even entertained growing close to, and now he's stolen my heart as well.

"I'm sorry it's so early."

"It's fine. I'm just not great company in the morning."

"I'll have to remember that. I'll bring coffee next time." I can't help the smile that tugs at my lips at his clear struggle with the time. It's nearly eight in the morning.

"I'll be okay once the caffeine kicks in." He takes my hand and slouches back into the sofa, cradling it on his chest as his eyelids dip closed. It takes everything in me not to crawl up next to him and snuggle against his chest.

That can come later. Right now, I need words to express how I feel. I owe it to Owen to be clear and honest about my feelings and how screwed up I am.

Owen leans forward and picks up his coffee, still with my hand in his, and inhales deeply before sipping the glossy dark liquid.

"I didn't think you took yours black?"

"Black and strong first thing in the morning, or I'd never get my arse up and working." He replaces the mug and leans back again. The tension in the room grows as I wait for the courage to set my words free. Owen seems happy to sit in silence until his body is ready for the morning. Each beat of my heart, every movement from Owen, sets the stakes higher. The pain in my chest intensifies as my anxiety squeezes my heart in a death grip. But it's not from fear. This is a new type of ache. One that has everything to do with the possibility of losing the one person I want to keep in my life.

My mind trips over the story that's in front of me. I trust this man. If that didn't exist, then I wouldn't be here. I wouldn't have gotten past the first few coffee dates. And if I trust him enough to share my body with him, to be intimate for the first time, then surely, I can trust him with the full story?

"I, er, need to thank you for rescuing me."

Owen swivels around, and he looks me up and down. No more tired and sleepy eyes. "Why? I was on my way to help even before I realised it was you. God, Ellie, you scared me half to death."

"I'm fine." I take his hand and squeeze it in mine, needing to get past the details of the accident and to what I need to tell him. "When it happened…"

"Are we talking about you nearly drowning?" His hands run down my arms before he rubs his thumb across the apple of my cheek. He looks lost as he searches for answers in my eyes.

"Yes. The weather changed. I got caught in the waves and took a bit of a rough time getting back to shore. But what I'm trying to say…"

"There was a full-blown storm. Jeez, Ellie. When you told me you went kayaking, I didn't envisage pulling you from the ocean."

"I know. But I'm fine, and Kez has already lectured me. Please, listen to me, Owen. It was you."

"What was me?"

My eyes widen in a stare as he interrupts. Again. I wish I never brought this up. I lean forward to meet him and press my lips to his, silencing anything else from his mouth. The kiss is soft and lazy but seems to work. Owen's arms reach around me, cradling me to him.

"Will you let me finish now," I speak around our kiss.

His nod is my signal to engage my brain again.

"I know I've not been the easiest to be around. I've built walls, and you're the only one I've wanted to let in, but even then, I've put a limit on by how much. After this, I don't want to do that anymore. You were the person I wanted to run to when things were getting scary. On the beach, I wanted you to come and tell me it would be alright."

"Ellie, that's what I want. God, if I haven't made that clear to you, I'm sorry."

"No, you have. You've given me time and space to learn to trust you and to see what I'm missing from life. It was my insecurities and worries that sent me running. I didn't want you to have a girlfriend who freezes every time you put your hands on her. Because even if that's exactly where I want them to be, my mind still likes to play tricks, and it's not fair to you."

"Or you. Don't think this is one-sided. I want us to fix

this together. Work as a team," Owen pleads.

"You don't even know why." I can't believe he's willing to overlook such an important detail. It's been at the centre of my past, changing the direction of my future, as if the attack was a pebble dropped into the pool of my life, the ripples still hit me again and again with no end in sight.

Until Owen.

"You'll tell me when you're ready. I know enough. I know how I feel about you."

"You have been so kind, so patient with me, but I can't control the panic attacks. I think they're under control and then suddenly I'll be back in that field with no real sense of reality."

"You're here now. With me. Remember what I said right at the beginning. I'm an eternal optimist."

"And you believe in love," I finish the sentence for him as my heart constricts in my chest and butterfly's swarm my stomach. Our eyes lock, and I fall deep into his eyes, safe in the wisdom that Owen will catch me whenever I fall.

Our mouths meet, both needing to cement this moment between us. His kiss is urgent as if I'm the source of his next breath. It's potent, and his lips work against mine, drugging my body with lust with each sweep of his tongue. My body weakens and heat flares around me.

My hands explore the muscled planes of Owen's back. His skin is warm under my touch and melts against the pressure of my fingers. The attention draws a low moan, deep from Owen's throat. It makes me feel powerful and sexy that my touch can do that to him. A surge of adrenaline rushes through my body as I take hold of the control that I have when I'm with Owen.

He's put me at the centre of everything we've done. He's let me make the decisions, the choices, and this time is no different. I'm in control, which feeds the lust sparking through me.

My mind fast-forwards to where our bodies are leading, and there's nothing but passion. I came to talk, to explain, but now I feel him all over my skin, I don't want to stop.

"Owen," I purr.

"I've got you. I've always got you."

His kiss is all consuming. Rich with desires and pleasures that I've long ago forgotten.

I stand and take Owen's hand, knowing with confidence that things will be different this time. He doesn't protest and lets me lead. My hands might have enjoyed peeling a shirt from Owen's back, but I'll have that to look forward to next time. For now, I get to run my palms over his chest. The fine hairs covering his skin tickle the tips of my fingers as I brush over them and hold onto his shoulder.

"You know, people could describe this as a form of torture." Owen sighs.

"I doubt that."

"Oh, I don't know. I'm holding out for gentleman of the year award here. Your hands on me—in my bedroom, knowing just how sweet you taste."

His words transport me into one of the romances I've so often lost myself in. The subject of the hero's ultimate desire.

"Would you like to undress me?" In my head, my words sound sexy and alluring. But I fear I've only managed to come across unsure and vulnerable.

"Yes."

I drop my hands to my side and wait for him to act. And he does.

Every move of his hand ghosting over my body spikes my breathing. It's like I'm a puppet, my heart and body responding to him beautifully. Thankfully, it doesn't take long for his fingers to inch to the hem of my jumper and pull it over my head, sending my messy curls in all directions. The static crackles between us as he throws my top on the floor, closely followed by my T-shirt. I can't look him in the eye, so I pick a spot, or rather a freckle on his chest and keep watch over it as his gaze burns my skin. Now we're even in the clothing department. Or close enough.

Even though we've technically had sex before, it feels different this time. I'm more confident. Sure of Owen and myself. And just as desperate for his touch.

The thudding beat of my heart echoes in my ears. The anticipation grows almost painful, but I know Owen won't move or crowd me. I run my hands over his skin and pull his body flush against mine. Heat surges between us as we kiss. This time I won't be stopping.

We finally release the desperate need between us and the slow tempo is wiped away by our furious hands and fevered lips. I want all of Owen, right down to his soul, and I know he feels the same about me.

I move us back until he's sitting on the bed, my knees planted on either side of him. There will be no pressure from his body to trick my mind this time. I'm in control. I hold the power. Over my memories and over Owen.

The tips of my nipples run over Owen's chest and send

charges of electricity over my body as I kiss up his neck and reach his lips. The pressure and ache between my legs only grows greater with every touch, slide, and kiss.

I sit back and look down at Owen. His erection firmly between my thighs as I gently rotate my hips. The look of desperation on his face makes me feel needed and wanted more than anything else in the world. More than his next breath. I know because it's how I feel. It's what he'll see in my eyes staring back at him.

Our hands fly into action, removing the final layers between us. We lie side by side. My leg hitched over Owen's hip as he pulls me so close, I feel the pounding of his chest against mine. The ache in my stomach is unbearable. "Please, Owen. I can't wait any longer. I need you. I need to feel you inside of me."

He reaches for the side table and has the condom on in record time. I straddle his lap and guide the tip of his erection to my entrance. Without waiting a beat, I press down and take him in one smooth glide.

"Holy…fucking…" Owen's jaw tenses and the muscles in his neck strain deliciously. His hands slide up and down my legs, and I can tell he's holding back. Being careful. Not wanting to grab or restrain me.

I take his hands and link our fingers, raising them over his head. Our eyes lock, and I hold his gaze as I rise and fall over his body.

We get lost in each other. Kisses against skin, moans of passion, our bodies intertwined to the point I don't know where I end, and Owen begins. Every emotion conveyed in the pages of the books I've read becomes a technicolour living dream under his skilful touch. Every touch makes me feel cherished, every kiss is intimate, every look filled with a longing that banishes anything other than him from my heart.

As we ride higher and higher, I can feel my body ready to let go. Ready to break free of the shackles I've lived with over the last years.

"Yes, please… yes… Yes!" My cries punctuate my thrusts as I chase the climax that thunders through my body.

"Jesus… Ellie… Fuck!" Owen follows, relief and desperation thick in his words.

I collapse onto his chest. Utterly exhausted but filled with a sense of contentment that is centred around the man beneath me.

TWENTY-THREE

His arms anchor me to him. They wrap around me like bands of steel, strong and comforting. My breath hitches in my throat, and he immediately loosens his grip. "Are you alright?" His sleepy voice is right next to my ear.

"Yes. Fine." As his arms relax, so does my concern. These arms would never hold me down against my will. "I came to tell you my story," I muse.

"I know you did. But I don't need to hear it." His voice tries to placate me, but it doesn't work.

"Please, this is important." Despite how mind-blowing the sex was. Or how needed it was, Owen needs to know the full story.

"I know. But I need you to know it won't change anything." He pulls our bodies up out of the covers and makes a space for me under his arm. My body nestles into him, glad to have overcome so much with Owen already. Now it's down to me to divulge my secret. My fear.

"I worked a lot of hours back in London. My job was great, and I was really good at what I did. The firm I was with in the city was growing. I had a nice house, savings, and friends. Everything I wanted in life. Everything I'd worked for was mine." As I set the context for Owen, I realise how much I loved my old life. The joy that surrounded me. Why I locked that out of my life here, I still need to analyse because on the surface it doesn't make sense. But I do know I have a solid foundation to build on, with the friends around me now.

"I was leaving the office late and driving home. Nothing unusual. The sun was setting, and it was a beautiful evening. The sky was lit up with a palette of pinks and oranges. It was almost blinding how bright it was. One of the roads took me past a green park area. Tall grasses ran up to the edge of the road. I heard him before I saw him. Loud barks. They were insistent. Desperate. And as I drove past, I saw him tied up to a stake in a patch of shrubbery." As I say the words, I can feel the evening sun against my skin, smell the dust in the air as I parked on the side of the road and looked around for anyone who might own the poor dog. My mind builds the world around me so accurately; I shiver at the fear of what will come next—like re-watching a film and wanting to jump past the scary part.

"I won't let anyone hurt you again, Ellie." Owen pulls me tighter against his body.

I nod into his chest knowing that his words are a promise set in granite. "In hindsight, I should have kept driving. But that night, I couldn't. That wasn't who I was. It still isn't. So, I pulled over. The dog's barks got louder, and I could see he was going to hurt himself if he was left there much longer. There was no one else around. The road was quiet, only a few cars passing, and no houses overlooking the area."

I walk through the scene in my head like I've done a thousand times before to see if there's something I missed. There's nothing.

"The dog wouldn't stop barking, even when I approached him. I was crouched down when the man grabbed me. A hand covered my mouth and pulled me off balance as I was hauled to my feet and dragged back farther into the grass. I flung my arms around, but it did nothing. I heard nothing over the constant barking of the dog.

"I was dragged for a few minutes, farther and farther from the road and into the tree-covered area. The sunlight didn't filter in, and I lost all the warmth that touched my skin. I knew this was going to end in one of two ways. I was either going to be killed or raped. That's what went through my mind the moment I felt that hand on my mouth. But it was worse than that. A clearing in the woods opened up, where half a dozen men sat, drinking cans, and starting a campfire. The jeers and hoots deafened me as the man who snatched me tossed me to a large man closest to me.

"Each time I was let go, I stumbled and tried to run, only to hit another wall of a man and be pushed back around. It was a game to them. I was their toy.

"There were times that night when I wished they would just kill me. They tore me, shared me, and used me in ways I'd never wish on anyone. But I didn't give up. Something inside of me kept me alive. Kept me going. They dislocated my shoulder from the force of them holding me still and getting too violent. When they'd finished raping me, they beat me, and at some point in the morning, maybe the following evening, they left me. To die.

"But I wasn't dead. I crawled through the grass to the road, where a passing car nearly ran me over. They stopped and took me to the emergency room."

Owen's body shudders as he pulls in a deep breath. My body rises and falls with his until I'm ready to continue. I'm not done. Not yet. Not until I've finished my story.

"The recovery was hard. The look of pity in the staff's eyes when they came into my room made it so difficult for me to move on. I shut my family out. Didn't tell them about what happened."

"Why not? They would have helped, surely. You shouldn't have had to do that alone."

"I couldn't. It was too hard. Too painful. The strength to verbalise the attack wasn't in me. So, I kept it as my secret."

"Oh, Ellie." Owen's arms pull me hard against his body as if his presence now can take away some of the pain of talking him through my memories.

"It's fine. It's done. I mended."

"But you've not healed." His comment is so accurate it brings the threat of tears. Running away hasn't healed anything, but it has given me the space I've needed, and somewhere safe to call home, where I can hide safely away from everyone. Now, I can see that tactic wasn't one that worked, but instead, gave me the illusion of working.

Kez began to pry my heart back open, so I could see the possibility of a life that was within my grasp. She gave me the support I needed. Until Olivia, or rather Owen, who made me take a risk. That risk has led me here—confessing the secret that has held me captive and to see the possibilities that are open to me if I can lift the locks around my heart.

"No. But I'm getting better, now. Did I ask you if you were busy tomorrow? I can't remember if I invited you to Amy's wedding?"

"I don't think you did. I've not been to many Sunday weddings before."

"It's not Sunday. It's Saturday. I probably should have asked you—"

"Ellie, It's Saturday today."

No! I run through the days in my mind and realise I must have missed a day after the accident. All that sleep on the sofa. I leap out of bed and search for my bag, finding it in the front room. My hand's fumble as I reach for the phone and I see the time. 9.27 a.m.

"Do you have a suit?" I shout to Owen.

"Yes, is the wedding today?"

"My accident, in the water, it was yesterday, right? Friday?"

"It was Friday, but you've missed Saturday. You crashed as soon as I got you home. You woke after a few hours asleep and spoke to Kez. But then you fell back to sleep. I left in the morning before you woke up."

"I missed a day?" My mind goes into a panic. I can't do this. I can't miss Amy's wedding. "We can make it. We can. I have to." My eyes stare at my phone as I plan what I need to do. I have some shoes I can wear. Kez loaned me a dress. We can make it.

I look up and see Owen standing in the doorway in his boxers. My eyes cloud with tears as I realise that I want to be there for my sister. Despite everything: how hard the last few years have been, how distant we've become. It's her wedding day, and I promised her I wouldn't miss it. And now that I might, I desperately don't want to.

Regret floods me as I try to see a solution.

"We have to try, Owen. Will you? Come with me that is."

"Of course. I'll drive. Give me ten minutes to have a shower and grab my suit." He disappears back into the room. "Better yet, you go to yours and start pulling your things together. I'll come and pick you up. It will be quicker."

With Owen's words, I spring to action, dashing back to grab my clothes and heading back to the car. My foot is heavy on the accelerator as I race down the winding roads to home. As I rush up the steps outside, I hear George bark and realise I can't leave him. Hopefully, Kez won't mind dog sitting at the last minute.

I fire off a text as I multi-task wrestling George away from me and running for my room. The dress Kez loaned me is hanging on the front of my wardrobe. I grab it and fling it on after a quick rinse in the shower. There's no time for hair, but I can't go the rest of the day with sweat and sex on my skin.

Simple black shoes will work with the plum coloured dress, and I grab a jacket as well.

My phone beeps and I pray that Kez can rescue me again.

Sure. I'll have George. Everything ok?

Fine. But I might be in trouble with my sister. It's the wedding, and I'm late.

The wedding is today? Wow! Ok. I'm leaving now to collect George. Save you time.

I don't respond but set about putting some of the limited makeup that I own on my face.

The barks from George interrupt my frantic panic, and I pad to the kitchen. Owen's standing, looking so handsome, and my heart constricts in my chest. I'm left staring at him, and it's a welcome distraction from feeling his gaze on me.

"Wow."

Wow yourself.

Time stands still between us as we both take each other in.

George's damp nose to my hand interrupts my gazing, and I spring back to panic.

"We are tight on time. Are you ready?" I rush back into the bedroom to grab the shoes I'll inevitably struggle to walk in and a black blazer. Amy asked for colour, but she'll have to make an exception.

"Ready?" I ask looking hopeful.

"George is…"

"Right. Kez should be…"

"I'm here." She bursts through the door out of breath looking like she ran all the way here.

"We can go," I state, looking at Owen. I don't have time to let the downpour of nerves and anxiety to get hold of me.

"Great. When are you back?" Kez fusses over George.

"Um, I'm not sure. We'll have to play it by ear," I answer and realise that I've not packed a bag or sorted anything out regarding staying over. My mind begins to spin.

Owen's across the floor and takes my shoulders in his hands. "We'll figure it out. Right now, we need to leave. Make the wedding. That's the goal. We can sort the rest out later." He nods, and it's easy to feel his confidence.

"Thank you so much, Kez," I call as we head to the car.

Silence cloaks the journey out of Tregethworth. Not awkward, just contemplative. Owen's eyes are fixed on the road, and I force myself to stare out of the window. We'd need to have the clearest, most uninterrupted journey to get to London in time.

"Stop it. We're on the way. It will be fine." Owen takes my hand and squeezes.

"Thank you for doing this."

"I told you. We're in this together." He glances at me before keeping his attention back on the road.

"Yes, but running off to attend my sister's wedding? I had some romantic notion that we could attend together, but not like this."

"How do you feel about that? Attending, I mean. You've never been too animated when you've talked about your family."

"This is different. It's her wedding day. I've been distant, yes, and that's put a strain on our relationship, but I don't want them to think I don't care." *Please don't think that.*

"You've punished them."

"Pardon me?" The shock is blatant, and I twist in my seat to face him.

"You left everyone behind after your attack. You didn't

share."

"I couldn't. I've told you. Only you." Hurt and doubt swarm in my stomach as his words sink in.

"Baby, I know. But to your family, they just see you cutting them off. No reason. They don't know what's going on inside your head. You have your reasons, but they don't know them."

I'm quiet. Still. Taking in Owen's words. He's not accusing me. Simply stating my behaviour from a different perspective. And deep down, there's nothing for me to be upset about. He's speaking the truth. He knows me and knows my past.

Over an hour passes before I respond. "Do you think I was wrong? To not let them in?"

"It doesn't matter either way. You needed to do what you did. You were protecting yourself and that, above all else, is the most important thing."

"I can't tell them, Owen. At least, not everything."

He doesn't answer but takes my hand back in his and wraps our fingers together. I think back to how I felt when I was in the hospital. The sad, pitiful looks. I was the victim, and I couldn't escape that, either inside my own head or to the outside world. Now I wasn't *just* the victim. I had a business, friends, and a hobby even if it wasn't always as peaceful as I thought. I was a mum to a wonderful dog and a girlfriend to an incredible man. Maybe, I could start to be a sister and a daughter again?

TWENTY-FOUR

We hit the outskirts of London after a swift journey. No hold ups, no stops. But we are dangerously close to missing the wedding.

"We're not going to make it."

"It's okay. We have time. When's the service?"

"Not until four. I thought it was a stupid time to have a wedding. All that hanging around and build up."

"Even if we're late, we can slip in. You'll be there."

My eyes skit between the clock on the dash and the little countdown to our arrival on my phone screen, it estimates we'll get there at twenty past four.

Dread curls in my stomach, its icy fingers gripping me and making me feel sick with guilt. We finally pull up to the stately home that's serving as the venue for my sister's nuptials. I don't have time to admire the architecture or design, nor the lavish décor as we skid over the gleaming, marble floor.

"Excuse me, the Carter wedding?" I ask the gentleman polishing flute glasses behind the bar at the end of the entrance hall.

"Down the hall and the room on the right. They are due to finish in a few moments."

Owen's arm serves as both my balancing aid and my strength. He's here with me. He won't leave. Nothing is going to happen. My breath catches in my chest as I try and gather myself. The tremble in my legs makes me hesitate to take the next step. Inside the doors, in front of us, my sister is getting married. I promised to be here. But I'm glued to the spot, too scared to open the door.

"You made it. Everything's fine." As if he knows I'm struggling, Owen cracks the door and slips inside, pulling me with him.

A few people look around, but I keep my eyes diverted. A row of empty chairs at the left gives us the perfect seats, and I send a little thank you that something has gone our way.

I focus on my sister at the front of the room, dressed in a plume of white. As I watch, I notice the other rows, all filled with people. My skin crawls with anxiety now I'm here. This is what I was afraid would happen. I grip Owen's hand as tight as I can, and he covers mine with his, wrapping me with his touch.

"You got this. We're fine."

The registrar carries on with the ceremony. She's talking about marriage before she hands an envelope to Trevor. They kiss, and everyone stands, including us as they both walk down the aisle.

The smile that I feel pull at my lips is genuine as I watch my sister walk towards me. Her beaming expression sours when she finds me. "Nice of you to make an appearance," she mutters as they head out of the doors that have been swept open for them.

The noise of the congregation rises as people exit after the bride and groom. I wait and see my parents leading out behind the bridesmaids. My mother barely acknowledges me, but my dad gives me a welcoming smile. The urge to get up and hug him overtakes me, but I keep that feeling in check until I can do just that.

Owen and I follow the procession out the door and into the reception area where impeccably dressed waiters balance silver platters laden with flutes of champagne and mulled wine. A Christmas tree over fifteen feet tall fills the corner of the room. My eyes search for my parents as I keep my back to Owen's chest. He's become my shield in the busy room, preventing anyone from knocking the paper-thin confidence I've forced in place for today.

"What do you want to do?" he whispers in my ear.

"Run a million miles away. Is that bad?"

"No, baby. And we can as soon as you mean that and won't have any regrets about doing so." *Damn him.* "Remember why you came."

It's impossible to grasp the why when I'm swimming in a room full of people; the alarms blaring in my mind constantly yelling at my body to move—to find a safer place. Owen is the physical anchor I need to stay here. And I hope he'll anchor me in the future as well.

The conversation we had in the car surfaces amongst the rising panic—about punishing my family. It was the last thing I wanted to do. The guilt that hit me this morning at the thought of missing Amy's wedding was stronger and more visceral than the thought of the fear and the pain of being in a room with a large group of strangers. That's how much this meant to me.

It was more.

"Is that Trevor?" Owen asks as I spy the groom, minus the bride, approaching. He's not quite as tall as Owen. Broader, with dark hair that's showing plenty of grey at the temples.

"Yes. Hi, Trevor. Congratulations." I don't move an inch, and I feel Owen's arm wrap me in comfort as he takes his place at my side.

"Ellie. It's been a while. And this is?" He turns to Owen.

"I'm Ellie's boyfriend. Owen Riggs."

Trevor shakes Owen's hand but gives Owen a quizzical look. The anxiety running in my veins fires up, and I take a deep breath and plant my feet. I'm a tree and can't be moved. Trevor's introduction makes me uneasy, but I can't think why.

"Pleased you could make it." His comment is fixed on Owen, but I know it's meant for us both. "I'm sure Amy will want to speak to you." He saunters off, without another word to either of us and I'm left feeling like I've missed something. Either that or I'm going mad.

"Have you met Trevor before? I ask Owen."

"Nope. I'm pretty sure I'd remember both his name and the arrogant air he has about him."

"Trevor, the toad." It slips out and before I know it we're both laughing at the reference. It calms me, and I realise I need to find Amy. And get a much overdue hug from my dad.

My plan to lead us through the room lasts for exactly three steps before I stop to take a breath and cling to Owen's arm again. He takes over, weaving us through the crowd until I can see my parents. The smile on my dad's face as he looks my way is everything. I break free of Owen and nearly run into his arms, throwing mine around his neck.

"Hello, sweetie. I'm so glad you could make it," his whisper is soft but full of joy. I release him and slip back towards Owen who's right behind me.

"Nice of you to make an appearance, Ellie." Mum's welcome is stern and tempered, just as our conversations have grown over the years.

"I'm sorry, Mum. But I promised I'd make it, and I did."

"And what would have happened if you'd have been a bridesmaid? Doesn't it bother you that you barely make it to your sister's wedding? The Ellie we raised wouldn't treat her family like this."

"The Ellie you raised? Mum…" It's on the tip of my tongue to lash out and leave. But then the cycle will only go on, or worse, I'll be left out of the family all together.

Owen's hand on my shoulder floods me with confidence, but I'm not sure I'm ready for a full confession.

Not now. Not yet.

"Mum, I'm sorry I left with no proper explanation. Please, please understand that it was necessary. For me. I needed to escape, and I know it's hard for you. Both of you." I look at my dad whose face is flooded with concern. "I'd like to hope that I can explain further in the future. That I'll be brave enough to tell you why, but just know that I never intended to punish you."

The look on my mother's face is a cross between confusion and frustration. But somewhere, under her stubbornness I know she's back in my room, pleading with me to let her in. To understand.

My words aren't enough. Not yet, but it's the first step. And that's what I need to keep doing. Moving forward.

"Change of subject. This is Owen." I make the introductions, and I can see my dad is pleased. His face is an open book. The exact opposite of my mother.

"Are you going to apologise to Amy?"

"Yes, Mum." My frustration with her curt tone builds, and I struggle not to let it affect me. "Mum, I'm sorry. I don't know what you want me to say. I've been struggling for years. I'm barely holding it together, and I need you not to make it worse." She bristles at my words, and I know I've said the wrong thing.

The bucket of emotions I've experienced in the last few days would rival the best romance novel I've read, and all of them combine to threaten my nearly calm and presentable exterior. My hands begin to tremble, regardless of Owen's fierce grip.

"Why don't we go and find Amy?" Owen steps in. He nods to my dad, and I catch a small smile at the corner of his lips. The thought of explaining to my Dad what happened to me—what happened to his little girl… Nausea rolls in my stomach and the iron fist of the memories that have controlled so much of the last few years encroaches.

"Owen, I need…"

"I've got you." Before I say anything further, he whisks

me from the room and out onto the terrace. The frigid December air freezes my face and stops the hysteria that's on the verge of taking over.

Just like at home, the fresh, open air soothes my fraying nerves. Or, it's Owen's soothing tone and constant protection of me. I look out on the manicured grass and take the freezing air deep into my lungs. Telling Owen the full story of my attack took more courage than I thought I had left in me. I know, after seeing my dad again tonight that I won't be able to subject him to that kind of trauma. It will ruin everything our fragile relationship still had.

"Shh." Owen strokes my shoulders and pulls me back toward him. "You don't need to solve all your family's problems today. One step at a time." Tears begin to burn behind my eyes, and I long to be locked away, back with George, hidden away from the world. The only change is that Owen would be in the next room writing the stories I love to read.

"You hiding from me, Sis?" Amy's voice rings out around us. The chill of the early evening is nothing compared to the ice in her voice.

I step out around Owen to face my sister. "Not hiding, Amy. Taking a break." My voice wavers, and I hate that I sound so vulnerable.

"Taking a break? You've only been here five minutes."

"I know. And I'm so sorry. The days… I had a scare out in the sea, and somehow, I mixed up. I lost a day." I see a flash of concern cross her face, but then it's gone. Back to the Amy who's so angry with me that I don't even recognise her. I clutch Owen and pray this won't turn out to be a battle between us. It's *her* day.

"I believed you. On the phone. You might not have been interested in the wedding. But I believed you when you said you'd be here."

"And I am. I want to be here for you more than you know."

"Well, it's you that put the wall up. Moved away, and don't bother to visit or stay in touch. What am I supposed to think?"

"Amy, I promise. There's an explanation. But I need you to trust me. I wouldn't have moved away and broken everything we had if it wasn't something I had to do."

"You've said this before. But then there's nothing. Months and months without a word. Why?"

Her question hangs between us, and I don't know what to say. If I leave her in the dark, she might never give me another chance. If I tell her, I'll ruin her wedding day and any chance of rebuilding. But as my mind goes through all of the reasons why I can't share, I think of Owen and Kez. They both know the ugly truth. They've listened to me tell my story, and yet I don't feel any sense of pity from them. Why did I need to spare my sister an explanation?

"Amy, I … I can't tell you now. This is your day, and it should be about you and Trevor and the start of your lives together. I won't taint that."

"But you're my family, too. You were meant to be at the front, standing with me, stopping me from fluffing up my vows. Where were you when I needed you?" She fixes me with pleading eyes.

The dread I felt this morning returns, but I have to give

her something.

"I… I was attacked. Nearly four years ago. I was in the hospital for a little while."

"Ellie," Amy's voice is shaky as she closes the gap between us.

"I didn't want to let anyone see me that way, or have to explain. Being around anyone or anything became too much to bear. So I ran. To escape."

"We could have helped you? We'd have been there. Jeez, do you think we wouldn't?"

"No, not at all. But I needed to leave. It's taking every ounce of strength, and having Owen here with me, just to be in the same room as all these people. I suffer from anxiety, panic attacks, probably depression. People or strangers scare me, new places, new people…" Talking about my feelings doesn't help, but brings attention to them all the more. My breathing quickens and my heart batters against my chest. But for the first time, I've got someone with me. To stand by and support me. I squeeze Owen's hand, and he returns it.

He's remained quiet, but I know he's there. My anchor in any rough sea.

"You're okay, though, right? I mean, you're not sick?"

"Just know I'm getting better." I wait for her to ask something more but she doesn't. "Is this enough?" Will she understand that this is the biggest leap I've made and I'm not ready for more? Because I'm not. "I don't think I'll ever be ready to tell Mum and Dad."

"Promise me that we'll continue this conversation on a day that isn't my wedding." She gives me a look that reminds me entirely of Mum.

"I promise. Are we good?" Hope fills my voice, and I wait for her to respond. She doesn't right away, and I wonder if the Amy I had as my sister four years ago is like the Ellie of four years ago—gone but always remembered.

"We're good. But you're not forgiven. There's a lot of ground to make up."

"I know. But this hasn't all been one-sided. You and Mum haven't made this easy on me. Christ, I sent you an engagement gift, and you didn't even acknowledge me." We start sparring like we did when we were girls and something inside me settles. It might take years, but I'll be able to rebuild my relationship with Amy.

"I'm going to get back to my guests."

I look up at Owen. "Would you mind if we made an early exit, Amy?"

"Seriously?" Amy's mouth gapes open.

"I can't spend the rest of the evening in a room full of people, Amy. I'm sorry. Maybe one day. It isn't that long ago that I ran out on Owen because the coffee shop we were supposed to meet in was filled with customers." I lean against his chest and wrap my arms around him.

"Just promise me. Or I'll totally stand you up at your wedding." She gives me a slight smile, and I know, that despite the limited confession and time together, our friendship is ready to rebuild.

TWENTY-FIVE

We leave the wedding without any farewells. The conversation with my sister was both cleansing and terrifying, and I couldn't take it any longer. Owen bundles me into the car and drives back towards the motorway. The first services we find, he stops, checks us into the adjoining hotel, and I collapse.

Emotionally and physically. I break down in the tiny double room. Owen stands and lets me sob into his chest. The kayak, sleeping together, the fear, everything that's piled on top of me rips from my chest and pours from my body in giant waves that consume me. Owen holds me, letting me purge all my pain and anguish through tears like I could flood the room.

Slowly, the flow of emotions quietens, and I calm. The silence of the room helps. There's no pressure or expectancy from Owen. He's manoeuvred us to sit on the side of the bed, and I curl up on his lap. The rhythmic stroke of my hair the only indicator of the passage of time.

After what seems like hours, Owen speaks. "I'm so

proud of you. A few months ago you ran out on me in a coffee shop before you'd even met me."

"I didn't do anything today." My voice is dry and scratchy. "But it's time I started. I wanted to be there for my sister more than I feared it. It was the same with you, to a point. Or at least with Olivia. I wanted to meet and talk to her more than I wanted to miss the chance." I sit up, no longer wanting to talk blindly into the room.

"And I don't think I've told you how grateful I am. We might have never met."

The thought of not having Owen in my life is paralysing. Step by step, touch by touch, he's courted his way into my heart. It's not all been fireworks and excitement. It's been gradual, yet powerful, like the change of the tide.

"What do we do now?" he asks.

"I get better." I look into the warmth of his eyes, and I know. I know, more certain than anything else about what I need to do. "Because I want to love you completely. And I can't do that when there's a part of me that's so irrevocably damaged." Owen's eyes flare to life and smoulder behind his gaze. "I want to love you with everything I am. Every atom of my being and every fibre of my soul. Or something equally poetic that you'd be able to write."

"Oh, I don't know. You're pretty good with words yourself." The pad of his thumb sweeps over my cheek, brushing a stray tear from my skin. His smile shows the dimple at the corner of his mouth.

"I'm serious. I know I love you. But I can't love you the way I want when I'm being held hostage by my trauma."

"Ellie, god…" He kisses my mouth, demanding and full of passion. It conveys everything I'm feeling, and I could get lost in that kiss forever.

"I'll take your love any way I can," he moans as he finally breaks our kiss. "And I'll do whatever you need to help you. Just don't do this alone. I beg you. Last time it was a mistake. I let you have space, and you ended up nearly drowning on the beach."

"That wasn't my fault, nor my intention." My defence lightens the atmosphere that's clouded the room.

"What I'm trying to say is that you don't get to do this by yourself. I love you too much. Getting to know you, falling for you, has been the hardest and most amazing thing I've ever done. And now, after you've given me everything, I won't risk that. I know you trust me. You've been in my bed, I've tasted you, and I see how brave you are. There's no chance I'm staying away." His words are more potent, more meaningful than reading anything he's written before. But it's just three of them I want to hear again.

"You love me?"

"With everything I am. You are the stars in my night sky, and the sun in my blue sky, and the inspiration for the words on my page. I love you."

EPILOGUE

FOUR MONTHS LATER

Is it ready yet?

I read the message from Owen and smile.

Hey, I don't harass you when you're writing. x

I'll remind you of that comment in a few weeks.

I'll let you know when it's up x

Over the last four months, I've been working on coming to terms, in some way, with what happened to me. I never sought counselling or even spoke to anyone about my ordeal. Only Kez and Owen, and that was after years of bottling everything up and ignoring my feelings.

I ran and hid. Away from the world and even myself.

After the wedding, things changed. I still go out on the water. My kayak gives me a sense of accomplishment. It's a reminder that I'm not scared to get back out and try again. And that's what I've needed to apply to my life. My anxiety and fear of people aren't going away overnight, although I've pushed through with Amy. We've been in contact most weeks. Maybe only a text, but the friendship we had is growing again. It will take more time with my Mum. Her calls are still frosty, but I'm not hiding anymore. Every day, I take a step forward. And when I stumble, Owen is there. Or Kez, or George. But I needed something more purposeful. Something to channel me. Kez thought I should focus on numbers. The business needed help, but with Alec's work selling through the winter, I didn't need to worry right away.

It was my love for words that inspired the idea of a blog. And it was a type of therapy. One that I could reconcile. My words might not make me swoon like the pages of an Olivia Wren novel, but they help *me*. With just over a thousand followers now, maybe I can help others as well.

I scribble my thoughts and feelings down and construct them into a post every week that I upload to my blog. I've even started interacting with a few of the people who've reached out to me through it. Knowing that there are others who've suffered a similar trauma has been amazingly enlightening.

This week's post has been the hardest to write. Because it's for me.

I relegated myself to the pages of a book. They were safe. I didn't have to interact. No one told me what to do. I was starving myself of life because I was scared of everything. My bubble protected me, but it also kept people out.

No family. No friends. No love.

But why? Why couldn't I have family, friends and love?

Step by step. One foot in front of the other. The sun will rise, and the tides will change.

And I'm still standing.

My dreams are now my own again. My scars show my victory, not that I'm a victim.

And a stranger can bring you the keys to your heart—if you only let them.

I might have thought that happily=ever-afters were for the characters I fell in love with, and not for me.

That was before I worked to make myself better. And now my heart holds the love for the people around me, but more importantly, for myself.

And because of my story, I know that everything from now on will be okay.

I click publish and text Owen. It was time to start our happily-ever-after.

The End

ABOUT RACHEL DE LUNE

Rachel De Lune writes emotionally driven contemporary and erotic romance.

She began scribbling her stories of dominance and submission in the pages of a notebook several years ago, and still can't resist putting pen to real paper. What ifs are turned into heartfelt stories of love where there will always be a HEA.

Rachel lives in the South West of England and daydreams about shoes with red soles, lingerie and chocolate. If she's not writing HEAs, she's probably reading them. She is a wife and has a beautiful daughter.

For every woman who's ever desired more.

Sign-up to her newsletter to receive
giveaways, news and exclusive excerpts
Join here: http://eepurl.com/bckw0r
Visit her website
www.racheldelune.com

RACHEL ON SOCIAL MEDIA

facebook.com/racheldeluneauthor
twitter.com/Rachel_De_Lune
instagram.com/racheldeluneauthor
amazon.com/Rachel-De-Lune/e/B00ZS3RVKQ
pinterest.com/RachelDelune
bookbub.com/authors/rachel-de-lune
goodreads.com/racheldelune

OTHER BOOKS BY RACHEL DE LUNE

The Evermore Series
More
Forever More
A Little Something More
Surrender to More
More Than Desire
Finally More

Standalone
Reminiscent Hearts
The Break
New Tides

With Charlotte E. Hart
Innocent Eyes
Devious Eyes
Vengeful Eyes
Forbidden Eyes
Tortured Eyes

RACHEL
DE LUNE

Printed in Poland
by Amazon Fulfillment
Poland Sp. z o.o., Wrocław